MW00416411

THE
CITY
IN
GLASS

BOOKS BY NGHI VO

Siren Queen
The Chosen and the Beautiful
The City in Glass

THE SINGING HILLS CYCLE

The Empress of Salt and Fortune
When the Tiger Came Down the Mountain
Into the Riverlands
Mammoths at the Gates
The Brides of High Hill

THE
CITY
IN
GLASS

NGHI VO

TOR PUBLISHING GROUP
NEW YORK

This is a work of fiction. All of the characters, organizations,
and events portrayed in this novel are either products of the author's
imagination or are used fictitiously.

THE CITY IN GLASS

A Tordotcom Book
Published by Tom Doherty Associates / Tor Publishing Group
120 Broadway
New York, NY 10271

www.torpublishinggroup.com

Tor® is a registered trademark of Macmillan Publishing Group, LLC.

Library of Congress Cataloging-in-Publication Data

Names: Vo, Nghi, author.
Title: The city in glass / Nghi Vo.
Description: First edition. | New York : Tordotcom,
Tor Publishing Group, 2024.
Identifiers: LCCN 2024024459 | ISBN 9781250348272 (hardcover) |
ISBN 9781250348289 (ebook)
Subjects: LCGFT: Fantasy fiction. | Romance fiction. | Novels.
Classification: LCC PS3622.O23 C58 2024 |
DDC 813/.6—dc23/eng/20240531
LC record available at https://lccn.loc.gov/2024024459

Our books may be purchased in bulk for promotional,
educational, or business use. Please contact your local bookseller
or the Macmillan Corporate and Premium Sales Department
at 1-800-221-7945, extension 5442, or by email at
MacmillanSpecialMarkets@macmillan.com.

First Edition: 2024

Printed in the United States of America

0 9 8 7 6 5 4 3 2 1

for Alice, a new world just beginning

THE
CITY
IN
GLASS

MIDNIGHT

The angel and his brothers came to the city
ahead of the storm, walking over the sea with
striped sharks following after them.

ONE

From the topmost tower of the observatory to the floating docks on the beach, the city of Azril lit up with paper lanterns, with candles, with girls throwing flaming knives and boys in firefly crowns, with passion, with desire, with hatred, and with delight.

When Vitrine first arrived, Summersend had been a fast, a time when the people of Azril kept indoors with black flags hung over their windows and ate dry bread dusted with salt as a reminder of flesh and the sea. Perhaps some, particularly devout, stood in the squares and mortified themselves with grief and goat-hair shirts, but it was a lackadaisical kind of fervor even then. Vitrine had looked into the dour heart of the penance and found within it sparks she could coax to life, nursing them over the glass cabinet in her chest until they glowed. As tender as a demon could be, she nourished them on good years and bad, on silks brought from Kailin and barrels of oysters from Brid. She fed the festival on her own blood and her own laughter until it bloomed like a bonfire.

Now, right before the end, the city threw up towering light and shadows as long as dragons, and the only remnant of the black mourning flags were the colorful veils that the celebrants wore. The veils were too sheer to hide their faces, but they spun as the people danced the old dances and the new dances and of course the ganli, so fast that they might leave death and sorrow far behind them. As Vitrine passed through the crowds, bells on her ankles and her dark skin gleaming under the torches, she thought of what she would write in her book.

Tonight, my Azril beats like the heart of the world.

She allowed a mischievous girl to loop a strand of coral beads around her neck, and she smiled at the grinning boy who offered her a skewer of grilled chicken studded with brined olives. It wasn't given to demons to bless those they favored, so instead she gave them gifts: an eye that would see through lies for the boy and the knowledge to tell good from evil and the ability to ignore it for the girl. They would not be good, but they would be interesting, and Vitrine reminded herself to write their names in her book.

She spent a brief while cooling her bare feet in the fountain where a half-dozen children caught the sleeves of passersby for candy and coins. When she tired of that, she went to rap on the boarded-up windows of the green house on Malaki Street, where there lived a shivering young man, the grandson of a courtesan she had cared for a great deal. Vitrine still had hopes for him, but they were of a different sort than what she had nurtured before he started to fear the open avenues and the broad sky and sea.

"Darling, my darling," she whispered through the boards. "Are you well tonight? Are you safe?"

A moment later, a voice came from within, guarded but supple, entirely without cracks.

"I am. Yesterday I received a book of stories from Valnesse and a pamphlet about the glass-winged butterflies of Noor. It's amusing—they seem to think the butterflies are real."

"Who knows but they might be," Vitrine said cheerfully. "Have a good night."

"You as well. Blessed Summersend to you."

The neighborhood speculated ferociously on what treasures the young man kept behind his boarded windows and his thick walls. Some guessed a fortune in pearls, others supposed ingots of gold gotten from his grandmother's estate. No one even suspected that he had kept more books in one place than any other on the continent, holiest and heresies and art and trash.

Five years ago, he had learned that he could not tolerate people, and so the stacks of books grew to keep him company. There were the slender towers of botany treatises as short and delicate as children, the fat stacks of romances that seemed buxom despite their corners, the stalwart disquisitions of war that could be used to build a fortress themselves. Soon, she hoped, he might open at least a window to the outside; if he would not leave himself, perhaps his books would fly out and live in the hearts of those who needed them, just as she needed the book that lived in her own chest.

Vitrine wanted that collection for the city, but the young man would not be young and healthy forever. She could wait for her library.

In the meantime, Vitrine amused herself on Law Street, where tonight the fools and the beggars wrote the rules while the august advocates borrowed their motley and rags to run drunk down the lane.

Vitrine whiled away some time encouraging the wise fools and the foolish solicitors, and then she followed a pack of masked women on their way to one of the manors in the western district, their smiles as plush and red as fox tails.

It was Marius Cantavi commanding their presence, and Vitrine fell to the end of the line as the women circled his private chamber under his critical eye. The women were from the one of the finest houses on Carnelian Street, black velvet roses pinned to their breasts, cheeks dusted with glittering mica, and they were like music given form as they waited for the wealthy man's decision.

Marius walked among them, enjoying the selection more than he would what came later, and Vitrine cast her blacker than black eyes at him, a sting of desire making him pause. Vitrine stood as docile as stone as he reached for her mask, but when he removed it, he found not the face of a woman but instead something beaked and snapping, the feathers crawling with lice and the eyes rimed with rheum and fury.

He shrieked with dismay, and Vitrine laughed as she left the women from Carnelian Street to sort out the rest. They might soothe their patron or they might rob him blind, and it was all the same to the demon of Azril as she tripped back into the streets.

She picked out the son of the Lord Mayor among a group of maskers, and sent after him a footpad with a lump of iron in a stocking. She had been on the tightrope about him for a while, weighing his courage against his temper, and in the spirit of the festival, she decided to let him stand the test. If he survived the footpad, well and good; she would see what might be made of him. If not, there were plenty of other exciting prospects to be found.

She rested for a while on a rooftop off of Marrowbones Square, the green slate cool against her bare back and one ankle propped jauntily on the opposite bent knee. A lithe gray cat came to investigate her business in his territory, and satisfied, he climbed up on her chest to purr his approval. Vitrine grunted as his heavy little feet sank into her breasts and her belly, but she scratched him behind the ears as his eyes drifted shut.

"Well, well, little lord rat-catcher. I remember your many-times great-grandmother, don't I? She would be so proud to see how far her family has come, and what a fine sir you look . . ."

Vitrine turned her head to the side as the cat butted his forehead too hard against her chin, and when her ear touched the roof, she heard the sound of crying below. It wasn't such an uncommon thing for someone to cry through Summersend, but giving the cat one last scratch, Vitrine wound her way like smoke into the house underneath her.

It was a heartbreak, and Vitrine examined the sharp edges of the fight, the hard words that lay strewn on the girl's floor like shards of glass, the way her tears tasted of hurt and of fury and perhaps just a little of relief.

"You are all made quite badly," Vitrine complained to the girl who lay face-down in her bed. "If you were like us, you would never bother with hearts that broke or took on poison like this."

In the end, because she could not take out the girl's broken heart and replace it with something more suitable, she only sat on the edge of the bed to stroke the girl's box braids. They were lovely, beaded with tight copper coils, and with every stroke of her hand, the girl's memories fell away, dissipating into the air like grave dust. Soon enough, the girl rested easily, and Vitrine kissed the crown of her head before slipping out.

The pleasure in Azril, she thought as she walked past a savage beating in the alley, was that it was not done yet. She had arrived clinging to the dreams of a refugee woman from the south, and at first, all she could do was hurry the city along, longing for the great spires and the royal greenhouses and the grand bazaars she had left behind her.

It had taken a hundred years before she was willing to slow down, another hundred after that before she went back and tore out some of her early efforts and refined others. It would never be lost Saqarra, which was empty even of revengers and scavengers by now, and Vitrine had come to realize that it never could be.

I don't need it to be, she thought with some satisfaction and pride. *It is Azril. It may never be finished, and yet it is still enough.*

Vitrine wove through the riot like a light-footed cat, and as she passed, people grew rosy with desire, drunk with love, wild with need for something that surely danced just beyond their fingertips. They did not know it, but they loved her, and she brushed her fingertips over their cheeks and their lips and their brows, promising them that she loved them too.

Before it was anything else, before it had a name or an observatory or the beginning of a library or a mayor or a demon, Azril had been a port town, and the tradition of the ghost ship was sacred. At midnight, Vitrine made her way to the floating docks with a torrent of people in veils, dancing and laughing and shouting with joy for they were no longer the dour fishermen and raiders they had been.

The ship given up for sacrifice that year was an old trading craft, the triangular sail rent into rags from top to bottom and a hole big enough for a large man to crawl through right above the waterline. The boys and girls of the town had spent the last two days decking the caravel out with paper flowers, and Azril's own master pyrotechnician had seeded the ballast with gunpowder and sprinkled the deck with the same. The small dishes of wine laid out across the deck would perhaps help feed the flames as well, but Vitrine knew that long ago, they had been for her, and she was still flattered.

Invisible, Vitrine stood by the pyrotechnician's shoulder as she checked the laden bags one more time, her burn-slicked fingers probing for any dampness, any obstruction that would prevent the blaze. Twelve years ago, the ship had failed to light at all, and Vitrine nodded, pleased at her diligence.

"That was an unlucky thing," she told the pyrotechnician. "Your predecessor hanged herself from shame, and I do not know if anyone who was there will forget the wailing."

Satisfied that the bags were dry, the pyrotechnician made her way back to the docks in a small coracle, and when she arrived, she nodded at the Lord Mayor's son, who was bloodied and a little shaken, but alive. He stood on the foremost pier, the arrow nocked in his hands wrapped about with an oily rag. As Vitrine stood next to him, smiling as proudly as the ghost of his mother on the other side, he held the arrow to a torch.

The flaming arrow arced through the sky like a comet. Vitrine watched it unblinking in wonder, and when it struck the bale of dry straw on the deck, there was only a count of nine before the fire started. Like children, the flames danced along the deck, crawling up the rigging and curling over the rails. There was a moment of almost peaceful stillness as the black water shone like a broken mirror with firelight, and then the flames found the charges of gunpowder in the ballast.

The boom struck Vitrine square in the chest, and as a dark billow of smoke rose up to the clear sky, she clasped her hands in front of her in joy.

It was only when Vitrine turned to the open sea that she saw the moon, setting now and reflecting silvery shards on the choppy water. Many things could come on a broken road like that, and then she saw the angels.

They were as tall as the topmost masts of the ships in the harbor, and their wings stirred with the winds of hurricanes. As a courtesy to the world they deformed with their presence, they went on two legs and reached out with two hands, but their faces were as blank as shields while crowns of flames spun about their heads.

The cry went up immediately, and in the chaos of people running for the safety of Azril's walls, many were pushed into the water or trampled outright. Vitrine felt their screams like the beating of wings against the glass case in her chest, and if she opened to them, she would crack. Instead she stared at the angels come to Azril, frozen at the head of the pier, and in a moment, entirely alone.

Arrogant, was Vitrine's first thought, that they would

walk so mighty through the world. Demons learned humility with their first mouthful of dirt, their first mouthful of blood, and angels had never learned it at all.

No, Vitrine thought, as the first in the line of four stopped by the flaming ship. It hurt to look at, too much, too strange, and too livid with grace. The fire of the ritual, birthed with love and duty from the hands of the master pyrotechnician, faltered with shame before the angel, shrank away from its greater light and its greater indifference.

Vitrine watched as the angel gently killed the fire, suffocating it under its hand as it passed by, walking the moon road to the floating dock where Vitrine stood alone. By the time they reached her, they had shrunk their visible part down to the size and shape of men, and they looked like men, mostly, though she could see under their mendicant robes that one bore the feet of a great bird, and another went cloven-hoofed. They were dark like she was dark but prouder by far, with shoulders never bowed by defeat.

"Will you give way?" the first angel asked formally, and Vitrine's lips peeled back from her teeth.

"Go fuck yourself," she advised the angel.

The angel's face, handsome, bearded, eyes sunk deep in his well-shaped skull, did not move.

"Will you prostrate yourself for grief?" he asked.

"Fuck your brothers," she answered, glancing at the ones behind him. They were even stiller than he was, as if he had at least something of the trick of seeming human and they had it not at all.

"Will you beg?" the angel asked.

"Fuck the road you walked on, the sky you fell out of,

the clouds that shielded you from rain, and anyone who gave you a moment of peace or comfort. Fuck *everything* that brought you here to stand in front of me without knowing what shame is, and when I dance on the wind, I will turn the names that were given to you to mud—"

"Enough."

Something flickered through the angel's black eyes, something enough like irritation that Vitrine paused when otherwise she would have kept on.

"We are sent to bring the city to the ground," the angel said. "We come with fire and with might, and so will the city of Azril be torn from the tapestry of the world."

Vitrine didn't believe him. There was nothing in her that could believe his words no matter what she knew of angels and their opaque purpose in her world.

"No," she said, shaking her head. "You will not."

The angel made to move past her, and without thought, she put herself in front of him, her arms spread like wings. He stopped in surprise, and she had to crane her neck to look up at him.

"Stop," she said.

"You know we will not," he said, his tone measured.

Vitrine swallowed, looking down at her bare feet.

"Would it have stopped you? If I had begged?"

"No."

Vitrine's hands twitched and when they came up, they were clawed, her nails tipped with iron and glowing hot. With one swipe she cut him open from groin to throat, leaping as she did so to knock him back among his brothers like a game of tenpins.

There was a moment of complete and savage satisfaction when she saw something move on their awful silica faces, that looked as if they had been hewn from an indifferent cliff face some thousands of years ago and never changed since. Now they were shocked and outraged, offended in their dignity even as their brother fell among them, and she came right over him like a hunting cat ready to cut and maul. She wanted to tear at their faces to see if it would bloody them, to reduce them at least to humiliated birdlike squawks.

Of course it couldn't last, and as the angel in the lead staggered up to his feet, the rearmost one who had not stumbled at all touched a fingertip to her shoulder, a look that might be scorn if he were not so holy on his face.

"Fuck you," she spat again, and then with a fingertip alone, he flung her into the harbor, almost past the smoldering ship. Vitrine hit the water with a force that made it feel as if she had hit stone instead, and inside her, the bones that she kept to better walk as a human among humans broke, smashing against each other like the sides of a ship struck with a battering ram.

She sank through the cold water, numb and unable to move anything save her fingers. In the beginning, before there were words to speak, she and her family had spoken with their hands, gesturing *food* and *hate* and *anger* and *new* to each other with increasing urgency. Now her hands fluttered with the sign for *no* over and over again, and it was only when she touched the silty bottom of the harbor, littered with broken clay pipes, bone buttons, and bones, that she was finally able to surge towards the surface.

Vitrine fought against her broken body, moving her arms and legs like oars, and when she broke through the surface, she was looking up at the sky above Azril. From where she floated in the harbor, the wreck of the caravel on her right and the ashen cliffs on her left, she could see the highest peak of the observatory, the slanted roof of the Lord Mayor's house, the elegant spire of the house of the courtesan-general. The city was still lit up like a bonfire, and from that bonfire four sparks flew up into the sky.

Like comets who found the earth too cruel, Vitrine thought helplessly, and as she watched, the angels, somewhere between their man-shapes and the giants of light who had come walking over the water, wove a circle over the city. They flew so fast that their flaming tails grew longer and longer still as they braided their paths together, forming a ring of terrible heat. It pulsed orange, it glowed red, and finally it went white and soft around the edges in a way that hollowed Vitrine with dread, that light that fell on Azril, crowning the city in inferno.

The heat sent a boom of hammer-like force through the air, smashing the water and setting it to a boil. Vitrine in the water screamed as her skin bagged on her flesh, as her flesh cooked inside her skin. If she was a human, it would have killed her immediately, but she was not, and for a short and terrible space, not longer than four breaths, she was aware enough to feel her lungs burst and her liver split, to hear the terrible ringing of the explosion itself before her eardrums ruptured and she could hear no more.

Before she was blinded, she saw the observatory tower crack straight down the middle, and she thought, before she could no longer think at all, of the quartet of bodies she had seen entombed in those stone walls to keep them strong and sound.

The water, hot and salt like tears, took her again as she crumpled into darkness.

TWO

Because it was written at the beginning of their world that they could not die, every demon knew the trick of bringing themselves back from death. They might sight the far flags of death's pavilions, but they knew they were not welcome, and for the second time in her life, Vitrine turned around and began her return.

Some of her siblings made the journey often enough that there was a strangely ductile quality to them, like metal which was amenable to being shaped without growing brittle. She had one sister who could shape herself a legion of bodies from a handful of grains of rice and another who could draw a real smile from sorrow. Vitrine's siblings were brilliant and talented, but she did not have their facility for remaking herself.

In the beginning, Vitrine was a glass cabinet, six-sided and joined at the edges with dull gray lead flashing. This was the hollow inside her that all demons had, and inside that cabinet was her book. The glass cabinet was more her than her dark eyes and her mouth had been, and the book was what she had chosen to put there.

Her brother, with dark curling horns and a bull's arch

to his elegant neck, filled the hollow place inside him with a river, and whenever she embraced him, she could hear it rushing over smooth stones, hear the lowing of the oxen that drew the barges along its continent-crossing length, feel a fine spray that covered her skin with the taste of silt and moss. Another brother kept a family there, and every few years, he added some son or daughter to the throng inside. When Vitrine fought with him, she could hear their fists pounding on his ribs, their voices raised in desperate pleas for freedom.

At the bottom of the harbor, she rebuilt herself from the ships that sank in the conflagration. She found for her bones the splintered and shattered pieces of the broken masts and sterns, and on that frame, she slathered layers and layers of harbor mud. For her hair, she stole the burned ropes from the ships' rigging, long round braids that swung past her shoulders, and by then she had hands and fingers that could sculpt for her a face, plump cheeks, wide flat nose, and a round and wise forehead.

Vitrine had no eyes until she came to shallower water, and her questing fingers found two marbles of black glass, frosted from their time in the waves. She put them in her head, and she was as complete as anything less than an angel could be. Wading out of the harbor, she caught up a shred of sail to wrap around her hips, and then she stood on the beach, staring at what was left.

The sun was just below the horizon, and the light over the city was a soft gray dream, a time of unreality where you might believe anything. For one terrible moment, Vitrine allowed herself to believe that it was not as bad as she knew it was. There might still be survivors among the crumbled towers, there might still be something living, something that remained.

Then the sun rose a little higher, streaking the sky with gold and giving the lie to her brief moment of hope. The air was heavy with the smell of char, and everyone in Azril was dead.

Vitrine's new legs collapsed underneath her, and she fell to the beach, still looking at the broken city and trying to quell the voice in her mind that refused to believe that it was gone, all gone, almost three hundred years of work and care lost in one terrible moment . . .

She was listening so hard for some sign that it was not over that she heard the crunch of footsteps on the friable rock path above her immediately. The promenade on the high edge of the beach had been a place for people to stroll and preen and to watch their ships come in. It was clad in stern stone, and there had been dozens of names chipped into the high sides where they sank into the sand. Now the blasted rock crumbled like ancient limestone, and the angels that walked along the path left cracked footprints in their wake.

Numbly, Vitrine watched as they walked along the promenade, virtuous and self-contained as the anchoresses who lived in the chambers honeycombing the northern cliff of the city. Baskets hung from pulleys next to the anchoresses' open cells, and daily, food and water would be sent up and their wisdom, scratched on little bark slips, would be sent back down.

Where they had once lived, Vitrine reminded herself, staring at the progression of angels. Her anchoresses had *once* lived in the northern cliff. Some of them had been women weary of the world, some of them had only been weary of trying to scrape a living from it, and some of them, some very rare number of them, had been actual mystics, writing words of power and comfort and command with thin oak-gall ink. Vitrine had never quite taken the time to sort each from each, so they were all special to her, all beloved, all perfect, and the angels made her think of their names written in her book.

The angels walked the promenade as if they hadn't seen her. They were already growing and changing, their limbs lengthening and their heads filling with light. Their radiance was a weight on her unworthy shoulders, and defiantly, Vitrine struggled to her feet, tottering forward so that she could at least be upright as they went by. She tried to find the strength to curse them, but her tongue and her lips were still too new for it.

All Vitrine could do as they left her city was stare after them with her eyes burning, with her nails digging into her lineless palms and her legs trying to collapse out from underneath her like a sickly foal's.

As the first vanished from view to some other place, the angel at the end of the line inexplicably turned. He was more light than human then, but she could still make out the smudge of a beard, the finely shaped skull, and the deep eyes. He was the one who had spoken to her, who had wanted to know if she would beg for nothing, and a cry tore heedless past her throat.

Vitrine nearly fell on her face as she bent to scoop up a piece of slag, but when she threw it, she struck true. The stone hit the angel's forehead like a bolt delivered from a sling, and his head rocked back sharply. If he were a human, it would have killed him, but instead he only looked at her through a veil of blood that rolled down to cover his face.

Vitrine would have shouted curses at him again, but their eyes locked, and suddenly she no longer needed the words. A piece of herself, some dark and deadly and spiteful piece, flew from her and into his eyes, making her a part of him, and for the second time in as many seconds, he flinched in shock. His face was bloody, and her curse would live inside for as long as he would last, which was to say, she would live inside him forever.

Vitrine fell to the sand again, exhausted, the furthest thing from satisfied, but she knew that it was all she could do. She would never be anything like happy again with the city pulled down in front of her, but it would serve.

She curled on the still-warm beach as the angels passed from Azril. She swirled her fingers through the sands, marking esoteric patterns that hurt her eyes. Behind her, the seas still pounded the cliffs, and foreign gulls had already come in from the nearby islands, looking for territory that had too long been held by the city birds.

Vitrine inspected the grief left behind. It was an enormous thing, and when she closed her eyes, it took the shape of a ghost-ward, a tall and straight post hung with the artifacts of those who had gone on. After the wars, they used to spring up like wildflowers in the places of the great battles, where the mourning came to honor their dead. They were easy prey for looters, however, and eventually they fell out of fashion, though it was still possible to come across one unawares in the odd corners of Imanea, where the forests were very deep and strange.

The ghost-ward for Azril would be taller than the tallest mast, and it would be hung with wealth from a dozen foreign cities. There would be lanterns dangling from its yew shaft and so many bones inlaid into the wood that it would have a dusky white glow all its own. Azril's ghost-ward would be the finest ever made, strung with jewels and carved with noble names going back to the city's founding.

It was too large, Vitrine realized with dismay, to fit in the glass cabinet of her heart, too large by far even if she removed her book, which she had no intention of doing. It towered too tall for her to begin to lift, and even if she tried, it would crush her indifferently under its weight.

If it were a real thing, and not a shape that lived inside her, it would be taller than the mayor's house, thicker than the girth of the shy and secretive mastodons that still roamed in the north. It would sink deep into the sand and rise up into the bright blue sky.

The sky is still blue, Vitrine thought, looking up. *I am not sure that the sky should still be allowed to be blue.*

One of her sisters could conceal the moon by sliding her lucky gold coin across its face. Another sister could, with one long breath drawn from the very core of her, blow out the sun for a few minutes.

Vitrine knew she was not as powerful as either of them. She could not change the clear blue of the sky to something more suitable, and she could not build a ghost-ward so great it would hold the depths of her mourning. Instead, she turned back to the city.

"Well, every moment I waste shall be counted against me in the days to come," she said. It sounded wise, like something her sisters Ashabath and Lili might say. It occurred to her for a fleeting moment that they would never be here in her situation, dressed in mud and ship's bones, crying with frustration at what was behind her and what was to come.

They never would have loved Azril as I did, either, came the defiant thought, and that gave Vitrine some strength as she made her way towards the broken towers.

THREE

Long before the city became known as Azril, a refugee woman stepped onto its floating pier carrying a glass jar filled with flower bulbs, and clinging to her green and tendril dreams was the demon Vitrine.

All of them—woman, bulbs, dreams, and demon—were freshly come from the fall of a great city in the south, whose gates were guarded by stone-winged bulls until the moment they weren't. In fifty years, the conquerors would leave it, and a few decades after that, so would the revengers. In a century, the scavengers would be gone, and in another, so too would be the ghouls. The city in the south would go the way of limestone, crumbling into the desert until nothing was left but an archaeological layer of dark gray ash and sorrow.

When Isra bin Khouri arrived, however, the city in the south was still a smoking ruin, and this city on the edge of the sea was nothing special. The people who had lived there first were killed by the people who landed there next, and they were in turn killed by the wave that came after. It was a pirate's nest with pretensions of finer, with stolen banners flying from the ropes hung between tall poles, the men and women adorned with polished jade pebbles and rough garnets. The children wore antlers of coral strung around their necks to keep them safe when they paddled their coracles in the bay, and the ships in the harbor unfurled sails of vermilion, goldenrod, and lilac, making Vitrine think of Isra's old greenhouse before the glass was shattered and Isra's family fell among the shards.

The woman Isra took a tighter grip on her glass jar, snugging it close to her ribs like a baby, and she disappeared into the city. From there, where she went and what happened to her was a mystery, but Vitrine managed to give her a gentle invisible kiss on the back of her neck just before she was gone, a blessing, a hope, a thanks for the ride out. Then Vitrine was alone on the pier, alone as she never was in the city to the south.

The sailors and fisherfolk dodged around her, knowing instinctively without seeing that there stood one who had been formed out of rebellion and rage, shaped by her own hand rather than one greater. She was a thing that had been pared down by pain until there was only a sliver of her left, and everything she had regained, from the top of her dark head to her gleaming black eyes, to her sharp white teeth to her brown skin hectic with a madder blush, she had made herself.

Vitrine's first steps into the city that would be Azril were heedless, and her next were doubtful. It was colder than she was used to, and the wind that whistled through the narrow streets was no kin of hers. It came down from the glaciers of the north, and in it Vitrine could taste the pine and the snow. If she drank too much of that cold, she thought it might freeze her from the inside out, and she shook her head.

The people were paler as well, with skin that was rendered white and red from the winds. There were fewer people who looked like her and the ones she had loved previously. Vitrine peered into their faces as they parted for her, all unknowing. She was looking for something familiar, some scrap of someone she had known before. She had known so many people, and she watched for their faces to return, washing up on the beach before the water took them back.

Once or twice, she felt a shiver of recognition, some eye or cheek or smile that she had known before, but when she hurried after it, she was always wrong, and being wrong stung.

Finally, Vitrine ended up at Gallowscross. It had once been nothing more than one road kissing another, but the rest of the city webbed out from it. The square gained its name from the scaffold built from old ship timbers along the westward side. The gallows could still remember being a ship, and in the wind, it rocked slightly, searching for the spray and the northernmost star that could no longer guide it.

Vitrine stood below the platform, stroking the upright timbers soothingly, and she took a closer look up at the three figures hanging from the beam as they looked down at her.

"Well, look at you," said the first, a man with laps of scarring across his right cheek. "What manner of thing are you?"

"Fine and mighty, whoever she is," said the girl with the pearl face and her hair cut short. "Hey, are you here to fetch us?"

Before Vitrine could say that had never been any of her

business, the third spoke, a narrow figure in a long kilt
and a hooded garment that covered most of their face. The
noose—woven from tough grass and wool fiber—sat over
the scarlet of their hood.

"Not her," they said quietly. "She's here for bigger than
us. Aren't you?"

"Maybe I am," she said, irritated with being caught out,
but before she could say more, a low drumbeat sounded,
the sound quick as a frightened heartbeat. It echoed
through Gallowscross, but before Vitrine could ask what
it was, it was answered by the high breathy shrill of a pipe,
something made from metal with a tin shriek to its voice.

Vitrine had heard plenty of good music in her time. One
of her sisters was made of it, nothing more than a tune that
leaped from head to head, sometimes given glorious form
through a viol or a flute, and other times only carried as
softly as a hopeless wish. Vitrine's sister danced through
a thousand years, but something about this song made
Vitrine pause for the fast staccato beats, the phrases that
were clearly meant to be sung and danced.

"What *is* that?" she asked, and the scarred hanged man
smiled.

"It's a song as old as the city," he said kindly. "Everyone
knows it."

"It's *silly*," said the insolent hanged girl with a sigh. "I
used to belong to the Sui Emperor, and such music we had
there. Still, it makes you want to dance."

"I should think we have had enough of dancing today,"
said the hooded hanged person sharply, but their feet were
already tapping again in the air, and with a laugh and a
sigh respectively, the man and the girl joined them.

An older woman with a handsome face and one arm that ended in a leather cap instead of a hand came by to light the round lantern hanging from the gallows. Vitrine knew that custom at least, that the dead should not spend their last night in the world in the dark. The lantern was made from pale green glass, and it sent verdigris light scattering over Gallowscross, the dancing feet of the dead, the ruts of mud, the one-handed woman's splendid eyes, and Vitrine's long shapeless white robe.

Vitrine held up her hands curiously. Through her long fingers and the uncanny green light, she could see, truly see, the city that would become Azril, and fatally and at once, like an angel would three hundred years later, she fell in love.

With a shout of joy, Vitrine leaped up on the gallows, and she danced with the dead, her feet on the splintered boards and theirs in the air. They could not bow to her, too stiff from their day's sorrow, but she bowed extravagantly to them, a final honor before they were picked up by the White Ship or the Click-Clack Hag or perhaps even something winged that they would think was an angel.

They were leaving just as she was arriving, and Vitrine knew with a burning passion that she would miss them so.

"Mine," she said, and then she turned to shout it to the city in a voice that could be heard only by the dead, the listening, and the cats.

Home, Vitrine thought, which was just another way to say how it was hers, and then wrapping her robe a little more snugly around her shoulders, she disappeared into the shadows.

෪

Gallowscross was still there.

It took Vitrine some time to recognize it, with the buildings on both sides torn down and the glorious mosaic plaza, turquoise and orange diamonds, broken to dust. It had not been a gallows in a long time, but when she put her hand down to the ground, she could still sense the sorrow and the fury and the grief there, far older than this contemporary destruction.

"Oh, but I am *sorry*," she whispered, feeling for all the world as if she had been given something precious and then through carelessness and neglect caused it to come to harm.

She shook her head, forcing her spine straight and refusing the guilt.

She had been given nothing. She had taken it, and it was hers to neglect and destroy if she so chose. Her family had learned that much from watching the humans that swarmed the world, that love could be a destructive thing. The angels understood love as destruction. She had chosen a different way to love Azril, and this destruction had nothing to do with her.

Vitrine knew she had a great deal of work in front of her, but she paused in Gallowscross. From the depths of her memory and the writing in her book, she could summon forth the old gallows and the three who hung there her first night in town. She closed her eyes, and she saw them hanging still. They had gone on the way that humans did, and they had nothing to do with her, but she was a demon, and therefore they were less than souls, but more than memory.

"Well, what a mess," said the figure in the hood. "No one will ever dance here again."

"No, people dance everywhere," corrected the man with the scars. "Different songs, different people to hear, but they'll dance."

"What did you *do*?" accused the insolent girl. "Why did you make them so angry?"

Vitrine tossed her head proudly, ignoring the weight of guilt that tried to settle on her shoulders.

"I didn't send fire to tear down the towers. I didn't turn a city of sixty thousand to charcoal and ash. That wasn't me."

"But you're here to fix it," observed the person in the hood. "That implies some responsibility."

"It's mine," Vitrine agreed. "Mine to tend, and mine to grow great again. Tell me what I can do for you here."

The scarred man swung one leg restlessly, turning in a slow arc, and he did not speak until he came around to face her again. His face when he returned was clean and unswollen, the way it must have been before they hanged him. He had been a handsome man, and not for the first time, Vitrine wondered why he had swung.

"We only knew each other for a short time," he said apologetically. "We died here, and we're gone now, so we can't really help you. I'm sorry."

"I think there might be white flowers," the hanged girl said abruptly, and Vitrine turned to her.

"Flowers for the dead?" Vitrine had heard that white was the color for mourning in the Sui empire.

"Flowers for *me*," the girl said, aggrieved. "No one liked flowers as much as I did, and no one ever brought me enough of them. I want white flowers."

"Might as well ask for an honest scholar," sniped the person with the hood. "Might as well ask for the heart of the moon. Might as well ask for them to play us the ganli again."

"White flowers," Vitrine said, looking around and wanting to cry. The dirt under the broken tile was blasted and sere. Before that, it had been city dust, trodden over so well it wouldn't grow weeds, let alone flowers.

"An angel could make white flowers grow," the girl from Sui said pointedly, and Vitrine nodded.

"I'm not sorry. I didn't tear down the towers. But white flowers. I'll remember."

FOUR

Azril before the angels came was known for many things. It was known for the silk and spices that it passed from Kailin to Combes and for the horses and brass it sent back in return. It was known as a city of license, which was to say, a city of freedom, and it attracted people seeking it. It was known for its observatory, its scholars, its sewers, its anchoresses in the cliff walls and its necromancers in the streets, for all the stories that the world told about it and that Azril told about itself in whispers and on its very banners.

Vitrine, if she wanted Azril back, could not start there, no matter how much she ached to see the banners snapping in the wind or the tall ships in the harbor. She couldn't grow an observatory out of mud. She couldn't even grow an observatory out of marble or quartz lenses or learned people. Instead, she needed to start with the mud itself, the river mud that cut through the plain from the west and the harbor mud that had come from herself.

The river was reduced in its banks, the clay baked to near-porcelain hardness by the blast. The marshland beyond the city was gone, and Vitrine wondered with brief bitterness what share the frogs and snakes and turtles that lived among the wild cane had had in the angels' punishment. Then she put the bitterness away and got to work, because anger could start a thing, but it took endurance and forbearance and patience to finish it. She was not skilled in those things, but for Azril, she would learn, and so she went to stand in the water.

The trickle of water flowing from the mountains was still warm from the conflagration. In what she was already beginning to think of as the time before, the water there would have risen up to the crown of her head and past it, but now it did not even reach her knees.

The mud shifted under Vitrine's toes and she could feel the dross of a few hundred years under her soles. They called the children who came to dig for treasure at low ebb marshfrogs, and mostly, they turned up bone buttons and clay pipes, the trash of their great-great-grandparents made fascinating by age and wear. Only the summer previously, a student from the university had found the diadem worn by Sophia Adare. Vitrine had known that Sophia had not taken her jewels and run to far Mato Lorno, and then the rest of the city knew as well.

She reached down into the mud and sloshed water through the handful she drew up until the silt and grit washed away. She was left with an old coin cut with three stalks of wheat, a bit of shattered worn bone, and a hairpin set with a small chunk of rough garnet. She tucked the coin into a fold of her sailcloth skirt, and threw the bone back, but she considered the garnet hairpin carefully. Garnet was plentiful in the cliffs by Azril, usually crumbled down to grit to grind far finer gems. They had worn it long ago when they had no better, and as soon as they could, they went about in starred sapphires and bloody rubies instead. No one wore garnets but those who lived on the flood-plains by the river, their shanties so routinely flooded out that they never cared to own anything but what they wore on them.

At last Vitrine fixed the garnet pin in her hair, and then she bent to put her hands in the water.

"Come on," she whispered to the water. "Come on. Come back. Don't you want to go to sea? Are you not tired of the mountains and the ice? Come and dance. Come and see."

What fire had seared, water could not heal at once, but it would be a beginning. Vitrine stood in the river, swirling her hand through it to make tiny eddies, little tides. The river had been there before her, and she wouldn't insult it by grabbing and pulling. Instead, she only called and coaxed, summoning it the way it wanted to go in the first place.

In a few months, a thin winter came, no snow but a knifelike chill in the wind and a numbing one in the water. Still she stood as the water withdrew, sluggish now and cold. She refused to be disheartened as she so often was in the winter. Instead she stirred the river with her hands, calling it, telling it how she missed it, and how when the people returned to Azril, for they *would* return, how they would garland it with flowers, swim in its depths, and be taken in its floods. Frost stiffened her hair, and she was like a dead thing stood in the water, no better than the shat-tered spars that stood in the harbor or the broken plinths stood up in the town. She did not turn to look at them. She was speaking to the river.

The days clipped shorter and shorter until midwinter, when Vitrine could breathe in at dawn and exhale at dusk. She was still, nothing but desire and patience and a chill that seeped into her, putting laceworks of frost over the surface of her glass case.

"Come," she said through lips stiffened with cold, and then finally, when the days stretched like cats and as the sky shed its gray, the water finally did.

In her bones, Vitrine felt the distant rumble in the mountains, jags of ice and meltwater come thundering down the hills. It was dangerous for it to come this fast, but she had called it very sweetly. Now the water rushed towards her, flooding its banks as it came, destroying the unwary villages up the slopes of the mountain and splintering the bridges that had cuffed it for so long.

Holding her breath, Vitrine stood up at last, her spine creaking like a ship against the wind as she looked upriver. She heard its rumble, she felt the way the world shifted to make way for water that demanded the sea.

The ice broke in shards from her skin and her braids and her skirts as the meltwater came rushing towards her, and it struck her so hard that she gasped from the pain and the exhilaration of it, cold enough to freeze her bones and hope enough to set fire to her book. She opened her arms and let the water tug them as if it wanted to tear them off her body, and all in a rush the river rose over her head, carrying her breath away like the lives of all the people it had drowned.

It was far from enough, but it was a beginning, and when she had had enough of the river trying to kill her in its great and wild way, Vitrine waded for the shore. Mud dragged at her every footstep and the current threatened to pull her under, but she only ran her hand through the eddying flow, as affectionate as a shepherd might be with a recalcitrant ewe.

It was only when she had gained the new shallows that she realized she was not alone.

The angel stood on the dry winter bank, hands clasped behind his back and his mouth drawn tight. She could see how uneasy he was, and she could see as well the part of herself that had become lodged in him, like a thorn set in the arch of an unwary foot. Her curse lived in his heart, twisted it, deformed it. He would have to live and grow around it if he wanted to live at all. She glared at him, still up to her shins in mud, and she spread her hands out wide.

"Well?" she demanded. "What else can you take from me?"

"It is not given to me to take anything from you today," he said, and she snorted. Angels could only speak the truth, and she still didn't believe him.

She gathered her sailcloth skirts up in a dripping mass and stormed towards the shore, realizing in just a few strides that her path would take her straight to him and through him. The force of the river's return had done something to her, however, and Vitrine moved forward, daring with her heels in the mud and her lowered brow for the angel to stop her.

He was every inch a human man, born in blood and in those violent days, like to die in it as well, flesh and water and bone and gall, and in that quick glance she could see beyond to what he also was, the pillar of light, the divine will, and the thing that swords dreamed of being. Vitrine was only what could be seen, though made of tougher and more malleable clay than humans were. She had no towering form, and what people saw of her, when they saw her at all, was mostly true.

She came up to the bank until only a handspan separated them, until she could reach out and take that part of herself in him back, until he could reach out and set her on fire with nothing more than a touch. She came close enough that she could reach up and touch him.

Then, as suddenly as he had appeared, he was gone, and Vitrine was alone on the riverbank save for the thundering water. The world was larger without his weight on it, she could breathe easier, and, her temper giving way suddenly, she did. She drew in deep, greedy breaths that had been stopped by the fear of seeing him again, and then her knees gave out beneath her completely as she sat down hard.

Demons didn't like to cry, but Vitrine rocked on the bank, her arms around her, her mouth open in a toneless high wail that burned her chest and clawed its way out of her throat. The first birds that came back with the spring heard her cry, and they fell out of the trees, stunned. When they rose up, they were streaked with white across their dark wings and their neat heads, a lethal white that killed every third chick that bore it. They were changed by Vitrine's grief, and it lived in them forever, the grief-stricken weavers along the river Rune.

Finally, hollowed out for the moment and tired of her sorrow, Vitrine rose up from the mud and made her way back to the city of Azril.

Angels or not, there was work to be done.

FIVE

The night after she decided that the city that would come to be known as Azril was hers, Vitrine ascended to the highest point in the city she could find. It turned out to be the roof of the mayor's house, which contained under it three stories, a venal man, a clever woman, a set of variable children, and assorted servants that were mostly up to no good.

She flipped to the first clean page of her book, and with a quill she borrowed from an irritated goose in one of the courtyard hutches and ink she had taken from a dead scholar in an alley, she started to write.

Year one, Vitrine wrote with a flourish. *I want my city grown taller, and I want more ships in the harbor. I want proper piers. I want the songs to be sweeter, and I want the gallows to be less lonely. I want the mayor's house to be far grander, and the house of the foremost courtesan to be grander than that. I want a tower to watch for enemies from the sea and I want another, even taller, to watch the stars as they dance.*

The breeze chilled the light sweat on her brow, and she tugged up the hood of her robe. Someone looking from the ground would have seen a nightmare shadow, something visible from one angle but not another, something that shifted to let the moonlight pass through her.

Vitrine let her legs dangle over the edge of the roof, her book open in her lap to allow the ink to dry. Absently, she added, *Find out if the people here can read. Literacy, then a university, fine as the one in—*

Vitrine frowned, blotting the last three words out with a careful pass of her thumb. She abruptly decided it was unlucky to name the city in the south. Instead she wrote *the world has ever seen,* and nodded with satisfaction.

The ink was the cheap kind, made from the galls of the oak tree and blessed iron nails. It looked black on the paper in the moonlight, but she knew that in the daytime, it would show itself to be brown. The iron would eat through the page, leaving pinprick holes and then carving out the spaces between letters the longer it lasted.

Definitely scribes, Vitrine thought. *And then I can have inks from Sui, the kind that blooms from black to rose over seventy years, and some from Padri, which can only write the truth.*

The ink from Padri was a holy thing, rare beyond measure and bound with the gum from a tree that had once been a god. It was only meant to be used for writing the sacred teachings of that god, but the monks were a trusting lot, and Vitrine was willing to wager that over forty years, they had still not changed the lock on the holy ink.

Yes, definitely the ink from Padri, she thought. *But not only the ink from Padri, for I shall want the poets and scholars to write me lies as well as truths, great lies big enough to clothe the city in myth and glamour.*

When Vitrine touched the words she had written, they were dry. She closed the book and brought it to her lips to kiss before she stowed it again in her heart. The ink and quill, poor as they were, she stashed in the bag she had taken off the dead scholar. They would do until she got better, and after all, they had been free. You could not get a fairer price than that, and she shouldered the bag, going to stand at the edge of the mayor's roof. Underneath her feet, the mayor dreamed of gold, his wife's dreams turned to a lover she had sent away many years ago, and their children's dreams needed no push at all to turn to red and bloody things.

"All right," Vitrine said out loud. "Year one."

The house where the Lord Mayor's household had dreamed so brightly was long gone, of course. Time destroyed things as well as angels did, and it had been centuries since Vitrine had sat on the roof and decided what she wanted the city to be.

In the intervening time, the house had burned down, been raised up, burned down, this time on purpose, and been built up and added to and redecorated and enlarged countless times. Throughout the years, it had stood between two stodgier buildings, houses of dignity and respectable origins built out of native gray stone, and to Vitrine's surprise, that saved it, or rather, saved a portion of it.

She was crossing the plaza, on her way to inspect the city's drainage systems and old cisterns, when she unexpectedly found more of the Lord Mayor's house standing than she thought she would, which was to say that there was something left standing at all.

The two stone buildings on either side had borne the brunt of the blast, crumbled down to rubble mixed with glass, and the newer gables of the Lord Mayor's house had been clipped off like wings torn from a bird, but the very oldest part of the house remained, a low room with four walls and raftered with short thick beams. From the outside, the walls still bore traces of the pale peach wallpaper, peeling now in long and shockingly fleshlike strips, and Vitrine hesitated against a strong and more than slightly mad urge to knock on the startlingly intact door. She knew it was ridiculous, but she stood with her hand on the stone doorpost, pressed so hard against it that the snarling lion carved into its face left dents on her palm.

Who will I find waiting for me? Vitrine wondered. *Would it be Hector Barca, who ruled so well for so long, or his daughter Mariet, who returned to take charge when he fell from that horse? Will it be the Tran sisters, who had no right to this place but made it theirs and drank wine out of stolen goblets and toasted to the robber god? Who would wait for me?*

She was almost ready to see them, in spectral shrouds or in the flesh, because some of them had been buried in the house's foundations and some kept publicly in reliquaries just like her own glass cabinet. When she opened the cracking door, she was ready to be greeted with pleasure and joy, she was ready to have things flung at her head for her part in their deaths. She found she was unready for the silence.

It was the Green Room that had survived, she thought

numbly, looking around. It was a particular favorite of the most recent Lord Mayor's grandmother, Viola Aquila. She'd only died a few short months ago, certain of her legacy and the place of her beloved family, which she'd ruled with an iron glove.

The Green Room had been her particular retreat, the furniture upholstered in green velvet, the rugs dyed deep green with moss and fixed with iron mordant. She'd re-sisted the wallpaper that had been so fashionable recently, instead choosing her favorite artist from Padri to paint the walls with leaves and grass, so realistic that you could almost hear the rustling of the beasts in the grove.

Vitrine took her seat in the visitor's chair, because no one could sit in Viola's own seat, taller than the rest and prac-tically a throne. She conjured Viola up as a hale woman in her early sixties, her own tenure as Lord Mayor behind her, but sharp-eyed and apt to rule if she did not rein herself in.

Well? Vitrine imagined her saying. *And how goes it in my city?*

"Poorly," Vitrine might have replied. "It is all torn to the ground, it is all broken. The river runs again, but what's left of the dead is piled at the doors, and there's no one left to mourn."

Viola snorted.

"Who has time to mourn?" she demanded. "Who ever has time to mourn? Cry while you work, and grieve when you're dead. You're not dead yet, are you?"

"No, not yet," Vitrine admitted. "But so many are."

"Well, they won't help you, then," Viola said practically. "Who will?"

"No one. No one will help me. I'm alone."

Viola rapped her dragon-headed cane on the ground briskly.

"This is Azril, my girl, the greatest city of the age. You are never alone here, and the lights will never go out."

In this room, in this one room left standing by chance and architectural luck, it was true, and Vitrine nodded. There was a moment where she doubted she could leave. She would only stay in the Green Room, sipping the memory of Viola's smoky tea and listening to her talk about the warring merchant families and ghost ships coming into port. She could have.

Instead she climbed to her feet and went to kiss Viola gently on the cheek before she left, closing the door behind her with a final click.

After a moment's thought, she touched the peeling walls and the room crumbled, a patch of green amid the paler stone. She didn't need the reminder, and she didn't need the temptation.

Viola and all her family were written in her book, and Vitrine went to rebuild the city for them as well as herself.

SIX

The winter freeze and the spring thaw had changed the city from char to rot. In some places, Gallowscross, the debtors' prison, Camellia Street with its elegant galleries, and Carnelian Street with its elegant brothels, the muck was almost up to Vitrine's knees. It was black, slimy with the spring runoff, and when she waded through it, it clung to her hems and stained her bare legs. Throughout the city, she could see sheaves of green grass and tiny white flowers coming up, and the insult to what had gone before almost made her dizzy with anger. It was new life, but not the life that had been there before, and she tore them up when she saw them, grabbing them in great handfuls to throw away.

It was a losing fight, however, as were the clouds of flies that descended when the weather warmed, and the enormous flocks of birds that came after them. There were her grief-stricken weavers, of course, but there were also rock doves come to nest in what was left of the tall narrow shops in Hyland Street and the dusky hawks that preferred the tanneries where mice and rats darted through the knobs of iron slag. The seawall along the lower districts had broken entirely, flooding out Capewell and Goresuch, and into the half-sunken quarters came the stilt-walkers, the herons and cranes that drifted the tips of their wings elegantly through the water and the black-legged kittiwakes that came to replace their red-legged cousins who had been destroyed in the blast. The gulls of course lived wherever they could, quarreling among themselves and laughing hoarsely in their new kingdom.

"It could be a city of birds, I suppose," Vitrine said to herself one night. She sat on the beach at a small fire, curled in on herself against the cold that had returned. "I could have an eagle for the Lord Mayor, and a siege of cranes instead of a council. I could have plovers instead of children, and doves instead of market girls, and magpies instead of thieves."

It was an interesting idea, but she hated it, missed her mayors and her thieves and her market girls too much to see them replaced with beaked faces and forms clad in feathers. It was almost enough to make her want to raze the city again, send great clouds of feathers flying into the air and streaks of thin blood down the towers, but she held herself back from it.

The next day, Vitrine went haunting the mansions that crumbled on the west side of the city, where the broad lawns had already begun to revert to thickets of trash pine. Vitrine pulled up the pines, throwing them down into the sinkholes formed by the hollow foundations remaining. The pines were fast and vicious, and if they were given a chance, they would choke out the beech and oak that she wanted there instead. It was hot and irritating work, and as she did it, she cursed softly to herself. It would be unlucky land after that, but it was fine. Unlucky people could live there, and they would make the people who saw them feel luckier by comparison.

A few times, Vitrine reached for a pine sapling only to find that it was a blackberry wand instead, studded with stickers and thrusting hopefully from the earth. They invariably bloodied her, but she allowed them to stay, along with the apple saplings that twisted from the ground. She didn't know who would come for them when at last they bore fruit, but in the meantime they could feed the birds and the deer.

Close to evening, Vitrine looked up to see a figure darting through the ruins of the Demorsico estate, so fast that even her very sharp eyes were not certain what she had seen. A moment later, she was after them, a stray brier snagging the skin of her foot and scraping it terribly in her haste.

"Wait," she cried. "Wait, just wait for me."

The Demorsico were secret sorcerers and necromancers, and their walls, built with their dead enemies and strengthened with blood and curses against those who would wrong them, had survived somewhat better than their neighbors. Vitrine ran through the doorway and darted through rooms that were open to the sky, following the glimpse of her quarry through arcades where fallen stone statues left hands and arms grasping for the sky.

They've come back, she thought wildly. *I knew they would, this city is theirs and they came back . . .*

She came around the corner to the bedroom of Avaline Demorsico, fifteen last year when the angels brought down fire. There was still a trace of faint blue paint on the walls, and a latticed window, nearly whole, cast strange and twisting shadows around the place. There was a frantic cooing echoing off the walls, and for a moment Vitrine flashed to the dovecotes, where the birds would return year after year even when the bars had been shattered and the roof fallen in.

There were no birds in the room, however, only a form pressed to the rearmost darkest corner. The light showed Vitrine a pair of long dirty feet and the strangely pristine edge of a lacy white hem. Vitrine recognized the lace. It was a pattern of exceeding delicacy, wrought from an abstracted design of ram's horns. She knew it well because it had been all the rage in Azril that summer, the one that she was trying very hard not to refer to as the last summer, and only the richest and most fashionable would wear it.

"Avaline," Vitrine whispered, because she had been there when the girl was born, her mother attended by a good-woman because Miao Demorsico did not trust the doctors that she was owed by her wealth and her position. Miao had been a raw girl from Kailin when she, along with a little help from Vitrine's finest pair of enchanted slippers, caught the eye, the lust, and then the heart of the eldest Demorsico boy.

Miao had been just what Vitrine needed to shake the noble family to its foundations so that it could build up from the rubble, strong as it was before but with the foreign girl's will and grace and unyielding temper. Even good blood would go to rot if it was allowed to stand stagnant, and from that ruin had come Avaline, the latest scion of the city to whom Vitrine had dedicated an entire page in her book.

She couldn't come to the town, Vitrine thought, her breath coming fast and hopeful. *She and Miao were fighting, and Miao had forbidden her from leaving. Has she survived here all this time, dressed in lace and eating bugs and frogs? Oh my poor darling.*

With a soft cry, Vitrine came forward to take the girl in her arms, but instead she found herself beaten back by a flurry of hands thrown at her face. The blows were too fast to do real damage, open-palmed and panicked, and Vitrine stumbled away with a yelp. Then, eyes narrowing and regardless of the girl's panicked cries and flying hands, she seized her by the soft arm and dragged her forward into the light coming through the broken roof.

There had been hopeful tears on Vitrine's face, but they felt like salt in the wound when she saw the girl's face. The year before, all the Demorsico, from patriarch to foreign wife to littlest baby, had been immortalized in marble busts. They were scattered through the house and the grounds, and of course the bust of the longed-for Demorsico princess had been kept in pride of place, the sheltered rose arbor. Avaline was a lively girl, but she had no special looks. She was sharp-nosed with eyes that were set close together and a wider mouth than was fashionable. Marble would never have captured her sly humor or her flashing temper, so instead the sculptor had had to make do with simply making her beautiful.

That was the face that the sculptor had given her, heart-shaped, sleek, and flawless. Like marble, there was something still about it, something fixed about the eyes, and it came to Vitrine that she had been made by someone without any talent for it.

"What are you?" Vitrine demanded, and the girl opened

her mouth to let out a warbling chitter, swallowed to the back of her throat and fearful.

Vitrine stared, because she recognized that sound. It was the family cry of the sandhill cranes that nested in the ornamental ponds of the mansions. They had been terrible pests when the ponds were stocked with calico carp, but now they were their own kind of nobility, stilt-walking through the shallows with their beaks held like rapiers at the ready.

In surprise, her hand loosened slightly, but when the crane-turned-girl thrashed to get free, Vitrine tightened her grasp again because she had realized exactly who had made her without any talent for it or indeed any love.

Vitrine stalked from the Demorsico mansion, dragging the crane-girl by the arm and slamming the door closed behind her so hard that it fell off its hinges. She didn't care about that because the Demorsico were dead, all of them, and it didn't matter any longer if the sandhill cranes went stalking into their house or if the bats flew in to nest in what remained of the ceilings. None of it mattered.

The sun had gone down, setting a sudden chill across the land, and Vitrine raised her eyes to the clouded sky and the jagged peaks of the shattered buildings around them. The girl squalled helplessly, and the cranes picking through the pond nearby raised their heads in alarm. Perhaps as recently as a few hours ago, they had been her parents. Now they only looked at her with their small black eyes, unnerved and afraid of the thing that looked like a human but spoke like a crane.

"You think you're funny?" Vitrine demanded. "You

think this will hurt me? You think this will make me think twice?"

"It was a gift."

The angel stood in the doorway of the Celindo mansion, his arms crossed over his chest. The fading sunlight gave his skin a ruddy gold tone, and if Vitrine squinted, she could make out the great wings that fell from his shoulders like a conqueror's cape. She shook the crane-girl's wrist at him, making her cry out again.

"This is not a gift," she snapped. "This is a travesty. It is a *poorly done* travesty."

The angel flinched, his shoulders coming up as if to ward off a blow, and then he squared them again with irritated pride.

"I was not made for such tasks. I did the best I could."

"Is that supposed to comfort me, angel?"

He was still, and she bared her teeth.

"It was, wasn't it. You thought your little birdie was going to make me feel better, would soothe me after everything you did. Do you know what would soothe me, angel?"

He tensed, all the warning she got before he was between them. He turned to face her, herding the crane-girl back with a sweep of his arm, and Vitrine gave him a mocking look.

"Oh, I'm not you. I don't need burning bodies and the screaming of children to put myself to sleep."

"I don't—"

He cut himself off when she stepped up to him, uninterested in the poor silly thing sheltering in his shadow. He was tall, slightly stooped over her, but she ignored the menace and unease that bled from him like juice from a ripe apple.

"I'm not you," she repeated.

No angel would have reached up like she did to touch his chin, to run her finger in a straight line down to the hollow of his throat. No angel would have folded back the edges of the slit in his linen neckline, baring just a little more flesh. Certainly no angel would have stood up on his tiptoes as she did so she could press her lips to the skin revealed, and then lick it.

He bore her trespass with a kind of wary patience, and, Vitrine could tell, he would bear the rest of what she might do to him the same way. He would *suffer* her, as if whatever she did to his flesh could compare to what he had done to Azril, and she stepped back in disgust, turning her head to spit.

"I can circle the world ten times with a thought," he said urgently. "I know the name of every sleeper under the sea. Uncounted armies have fallen under my sword, and I raised the mountains of Edah to the skies. Tell me what would soothe you."

"You have nothing I want," she told him, and he rubbed one hand hard over the center of his chest.

"The piece of you in me burns. I cannot remove it no matter what I cut, and my brothers will not allow me to return while I have it."

"Good."

She could feel his eyes on her, all of them, seeing her in every way he could. He could see the small body she inhabited, he could see her birthed form, a five-hundred-year storm that tore across the desert in a rage before it was bound in flesh by her crying parent. He could see the glass case inside her, and she guessed that he could see the book she kept inside it as well.

Perhaps he also saw the fury that ate at her ever-renewing flesh, and how if she allowed it to, it would consume her and even the memory of the city she loved. Perhaps that was why he nodded stiffly, defeated.

"Now you see. Let me take care of the stupid thing you have created, if you have not the strength to do it."

She expected him to step aside ashamed, let her snap the poor crane-girl's neck, but instead he straightened and shook his head.

"No. She is my mistake."

Curious, she watched as he turned away from her, his wings coming up and spreading out to grant them some privacy. The crane-girl made a crooning hesitant sound that ended with a brisk wet snap, and then he turned with her in his arms. With her long hair covering her face, she looked more like Avaline, and the demon steeled her heart. One more dead thing, what was that? Her loved ones were gone, and she would waste no tears for an angel's foolishness.

"Lay her down here."

Deliberately, Vitrine turned away from him, going to gather the slats of dry wood that had once been elegant dulcimers and paintings bright with egg tempera. They had escaped his fire but not hers, and as the sun set down behind the hills, she built a tidy pyramid of wood and lit it with a tinderbox she found somehow intact in the rubble. Over it, she balanced some rocks and a window shutter of curlicue iron to serve as an impromptu grill.

The angel watched with hollow eyes as she stripped away the crane-girl's muddied dress and bared white flesh to the emerging moon. She jointed her at the shoulders, the elbows, and the knees, laying her limbs on the iron so that the flesh crisped and the fat dripped richly onto the coals. The rest would require more careful butchering, which she did not care to do, and she left it to sit on the grass, still terribly recognizable for what it was: a mutilation and an angel's error.

She tasted like crane, all fish and frog and snail rather than human, and to her, Vitrine added ramps and mustard that had grown in the angels' despite.

❦

She ate delicately, relishing the angel's dark gaze, blotting the grease from her mouth with her fingertips.

"Will you be welcome to my fire, angel?" she asked, holding out the crossed bones of the crane girl's forearm invitingly.

"You did not have to do this," the angel said, and the smile fell from her face.

"Of course I did. Do you see? You can offer me nothing I want. You can give me nothing so precious that I will hesitate to destroy it. You will not be suffered in this city. You will not be welcomed, you will not be tolerated. The buildings will not shelter you and the fountains will run dry when you reach for the water."

"Another curse?" asked the angel wearily, and she shook her head.

"Only a declaration. You already bear the worst of what I can give."

He nodded, his eyes closing briefly from the pain of the truth, but he did not fade back into the darkness. Instead he sat with her at the fire; vigil, she supposed, for his poor misbegotten girl. Vitrine ate her slowly, watching the angel as she did so. She was grudgingly impressed when he did not flinch, not even when she took the girl's long black plait and laid it neatly atop her remains.

"She deserves a burial."

Vitrine shrugged.

"Then bury her if you like, or leave her for the harriers. You've made such a mess of her that one is as appropriate as another."

A spasm of distaste crossed the angel's face. Perhaps his kind did not have a great deal of experience with this end of things. They were the heralds of the dawn, when things awakened and were made new, and they came at the end. It occurred to Vitrine that they did not have experience with what came after the end, when everything was over and ruined.

"Don't you know that sometimes you can walk away from the end?" she asked almost gently, and the look he gave her was dark.

Her belly full, Vitrine doused the fire and stood. There was nothing left to say to the angel, so she went off in the dark, but for some reason she did not entirely understand, she did not go far. Instead she slipped into the wind, hitching a ride with a firefly. The night lit up with strange colors, and she flew along behind the angel, who shone with cool blues and soft silvers. To the firefly, the angel had two enormous clusters of eyes on either side of his head, so numerous and small they looked almost velvety, and the colors he flashed, over and over again like a signal waiting for the one person who needed to see it, spoke *holy and holy and holy.*

She flew behind him as he made his way through the disintegrating mansions, and then greatly daring, she settled on the seam of his tunic, grabbing on to the linen. This close, with her borrowed eyes, she could see the sheen of sweat on his throat, and the crinkling hairs of his beard. He breathed uneasily as one unused to it, and there was a faint glow in the swirls of air leaving his lips.

He came to the small graveyard that had once been the sole provenance of the Mercer family. The wall that kept in their dead was gone, and with it the great compass that had been engraved upon it. The Mercers were wild, merchant princesses and razor-tongued diplomats bred from pirate stock, and the only reason that they were no longer buried in silk shrouds at sea was because generations ago, the first Malabec Mercer had fallen in love with Azril and committed her entire family to its gates.

Now the Mercers were gone, and though the family was far-flung with members on the sea as well as in the courts of Brokkslevan and Yfs, they were not *her* Mercers, and they did not matter. The mausoleums were shattered and the old dry bones, unmixed with flesh or fat, burned a pure layer of black charcoal into the ground. Settled on the spar of a broken pine sapling, Vitrine watched as the angel knelt in the dirt and hollowed out a hole with his broad hands. First he had to get through the broken bits of crypt, and then came the layer of bone. Underneath that was the clay soil, harsh and fit only for the planting of bodies and sorrow.

As he dug, Vitrine watched with interest as the angel's shoulders shook. She wondered if his kind, so set on how perfect they were allowed to make the world, could cry, and if so, what emotion might move him to it. She wondered if he considered his crane-girl a murder or merely some failed experiment.

Finally, the angel lowered the bundle of ruin and hair into the hole and covered it up again. Against the odds, he found an intact slab of stone as large as a shield, part of the fourth Malabec's own tomb. He laid it over the little grave he had made, tamping it down with gentle taps to embed it firmly in the clay, and then he climbed to his feet again, standing with his hands clasped before him.

He stood there long enough that Vitrine grew bored, winging her way through the night to haunt the ruined streets and broken squares.

Maybe he'll stay there forever as her memorial, she thought spitefully. *He can stand there for all of them if he's really sorry.*

SEVEN

Vitrine knew in a practical way that Azril was not special. Perhaps a thousand years ago, it would have been, the triumph of some horselord or seaqueen, some wonder of resources and accord and luck that managed to get that many people living in one place without tearing each other to pieces. A city took all those things and then time, and it wasn't as if there was any shortage of that.

Azril was not special, but it was unique just like all the rest, and so Vitrine cleared the streets, taking up a spade and beginning by the shore. The buildings had fallen like so many careless drunk girls, casting glass that glittered like jewels into the broad avenues, obscuring the white pavers that divided the boulevards down the center.

Azril's first streets were narrow and haphazard, like a handful of straw thrown onto the ground. There had been a revolt some decades ago, a surprise, but not, Vitrine thought in retrospect, a terrible thing, for all it had briefly turned Gallowscross into a killing floor. The blood there ran three fingers deep, and the severed heads slowly mummified in the salt air.

Those that came after learned their lessons well regarding rule of law and how far a people could be pushed, and also about how easily a single household could be turned inside out to barricade a street. They rebuilt after the fires with an eye for wide roads, the main ones broad enough at least to allow two coaches to pass side by side, the small ones large enough for a vegetable cart.

It was an architect from Gao who had designed the city as it was now, the streets as straight as virtue, the squares built on some astrological design rather than on where someone's mule had died or where they hung their thieves. He had come to Azril after doing the work of a king too well, and he loved the city, old and new, almost as much as Vitrine did. When he died, Vitrine honored his last wish and stole his body from where it lay in the small Gaoese cemetery to bury it under Palavar Square, where he could rejoice forever in the tight fit of the paver stones and the feet walking his streets.

Vitrine didn't need to sleep or to eat, and before the fall came again, she had cleared the way from the shore up to the doors of the Lord Mayor's house. Sitting on the steps with her back to the ruin, she could see the way she had come, and if she half-closed her eyes, she could imagine the people in the streets still, the setting sun giving them shadows as long as mourning veils. She did not imagine them decked out for Summersend, but instead as they were through the centuries since she had come to Azril, passing through on their way somewhere else or, like her, finding the place where they would stay.

The longer she sat, the clearer their faces became, and she smiled to see her old friends, the rogues, the strange ones, the geniuses, and the criminals. Some of them had done very well for themselves by the end, others not so much. Some of them smiled and waved at her, while others spat on the ground between them, making the sign against the evil eye with their thumb thrust up between their fingers. Most of them blinked at her as if they recognized her from some dream or vision, something that faded as soon as they awakened.

The parade of ghosts continued, as long as the history of Azril was long and as short, and at the very end of it was a tall and gaunt young man, his beard and mustache cut perfectly, and his eyes piercing like arrows into a saint's body. He glared at her, and Vitrine rose up in shock from the sight of him, for he had loved the city almost as much as she had, and he had been sent away from it, never to return.

Oh, he came back, she thought in shock, running after the procession. *He came back and he found it as dead as he was.*

She ran after them as they went before her, their languid movements somehow entirely outpacing her legendary quickness. Sometimes, the man at the end would turn to look at her, and she could see there a fury identical to her own.

You did not watch it well enough, his gaze told her. *You did not protect it. You did not defend it, and so it is gone.*

She would catch him. She would explain. She would bring it all back, from the chicken coops in the small tight yards of the clay workers' quarter to the sapphires that were hidden in the Fleetfox well.

But please, I cannot do it without you, she thought, and it wasn't just the young man with the immaculate beard anymore. She was talking to all of them, because it would not be, would never be Azril without them, and she could not bear it.

She ran after them, and just when she drew close, just when she knew that a lunge would let her catch his sleeve, would allow her to turn him so she could explain it all, both the destruction and his exile, strong arms wrapped around her waist, dragging her back and then, with a single flap of great gray wings, up into the air.

Vitrine stared down at the space where the ghost parade had been just a moment before, for they were gone as if they had never been. There was only ruin in front of her and an angel behind, and she dug her sharp nails into the arm that held her, drawing blood with a furious cat's hiss.

The angel didn't swear but he drew a hard breath at the pain of being torn. For a moment, Vitrine thought he was going to drop her, but instead, he wheeled around, clutching her harder to him as he turned.

"Put me down," she shouted as he gained speed and height, but he ignored her even as she clawed him down to the bone. His blood, more gold than gold and more precious by far, spilled gleaming to the darkening ruins below. Where it fell the ground was blessed, and Vitrine howled at the thought of her city being in any way favored by the one that had destroyed it.

No matter how she struggled, she could not escape from the angel's grasp, and her lungs strained as he ascended. It was his place and not hers, angels made for the thinner air of the condors and the bustards, carrion-eaters all. Vitrine gasped, unable to shout, and he went higher still, up into the empty blue of the sky. It was so empty, she thought, her head throbbing and her skin almost blistering with cold.

Was this what he had come from? Was this what was inside him while her family filled themselves with a riot of wealth and pleasure? No wonder he was the thing he was.

"Look," he called finally. "Look down, and see."

And for a moment she did. He had gone so high that first her eyes could only fall on the sea that lapped the coast, how the line of the water met with perfect love the blue of the sky, and how in its vastness it curved down. The light was clearer than the glass of her cabinet and so bright it threatened to mend the cracks that ran her through. For a single moment, she could truly see the size of the world and how far it went. She could travel so far without ever seeing a thing that she had seen before. In a world so large, you could run from anything, and Vitrine's grief threatened to flee.

She wrestled it back to her like it was a child running into a busy street, snarling and protective because now she could see the angel's ploy.

She turned herself into a tiger, twisting her head to bite down on his shoulder, but he only took her by the loose skin at the back of her neck. She swung like a kitten in her mother's teeth before she twisted into a serpent, looping her thick body up and over the angel's shoulders, twining herself around him in an embrace that grew tighter and tighter yet. He bore her until he could no longer, and then he unwound her tail-first as neatly as he might untangle a child's game of spiderwebs.

She was a human again, turning in his arms so that he had to hold her tight, chest to chest. They were no more their bodies than a jar of seawater is the ocean, but still their bodies were not nothing. His eyes, Vitrine saw, were as dark as hers liked to be. This close, she could see through them the fire that animated him, back to the forge where adamantine and obedience alike had been hammered into a divine weapon.

I could put it out, Vitrine thought, momentarily enchanted. *I could reach through them to that fire and I could burn myself until my ashes mingled with what he was and he would never be an angel again.*

Perhaps he understood her, because he shut his eyes, shuttered them behind bruised-looking eyelids and a fan of long, lush eyelashes. It would not have stopped her, but with that holy part of him hidden, he was beautiful, and her mouth went dry.

Not one in my family has ever kissed one of his.

Instantly, the thought revolted her, both for what it was and that she had thought it at all. She bit him instead, lunging forward like that tiger she had been. She bit him high on his right cheek, hard enough her teeth knocked against the bone underneath. It was a real bite, nothing behind it but teeth and muscle, nothing that could damage an angel, but still he cried out, surprised enough to let her go.

She spread her arms. In a moment, she would be an eagle or a bat, but now she was falling and free.

This time he had to stoop like a hawk to catch her before she struck the ground, and then she was in his arms once more, hissing and knitting her nails into the wounds she had made previously. It must have hurt a great deal, but he only kept falling, flaring his wings at the last moment to land and set her carefully on the ground.

"You must not follow the dead. You are not one of them, you must not walk as they do."

She glared at him as only a city cat could glare, and

then she exhaled, sitting tailor fashion among the ruins of a garden. She peered up at him from among the stalks of pennyweed and honeybelle gone tall and feral, lifting her chin proudly.

"There was no danger," she said. "They were my people, all of them. They wouldn't harm me. They couldn't."

"And do you keep your knives so dull that they would never cut you?" asked the angel sharply, but then he shook his head at once.

"That is not how I wished to begin," he said, and she climbed to her feet, brushing the dust from her skirts.

"Do not begin at all," she told him. "I might have walked after the dead and been very happy."

"Their city is not your city," the angel countered. "You wouldn't have been."

She ignored the fact that he was likely right, and looked around the garden, still bounded by the remnants of a high wall. The walls had been reduced to rubble, of course, but there was still a mostly intact column of green stone, the pedestal for some guardian statue. Vitrine remembered that it had been an angel; scattered on the ground, she could discern the fraction of a sword, a few fingers so carefully detailed and separate that they looked horrifyingly lifelike pushing out of the debris.

A few generations ago, it had been nothing but the humble greenhouse of a young woman who had come overland with a large store of seeds. She had absolutely no memory at all of where they or she had come from. She took her name from a ship she had sailed on, and that night, unpacking her bag with trembling fingers, she removed the bulbs wrapped carefully in paper, the seeds folded in paper packets, the small signature of pages sewn together and containing recipes for fertilizer and compost, lists of the seeds that loved winter and lists of the bulbs she would have to treat like the most delicate of southern princes. At the last, she pulled out a bloody knife wrapped in a scrap of stained green silk, and this she laid with the rest, wondering who she had taken it from.

She didn't remember whose blood was on the knife, but she knew how to grow plants, so that was what she did. She grew them first in cracked pots and horse troughs, then behind the temple she cleaned for food, shelter, and the loan of a small bit of earth in its shadow. Finally, close to a well and in good sunlight, there was a patch of land that Vitrine cleared out for her. What had been there before failed to please, and after Vitrine carefully set it alight, the soil was left with a rich layer of ash and regret.

"This was a bookbinder's once," Vitrine found herself saying. "Then it was a greenhouse, and then it was a ruin."

The angel looked around with a frown, taking in the pipeweed and jewelknot that grew up out of the ground around them. They were common plants and hardy. Though angels might sing a blessing for every blade of grass and every pebble, it was hard to imagine an angel patient enough to sing for weeds.

"This isn't my work," he said gruffly, and Vitrine shook her head.

"No, it wasn't. This was spoiled before you came. You were too late for this one."

"Who ruined it?"

"The woman who built it up and then set it on fire when she remembered what it was for. She did, eventually. My precious Chanda could not forget forever. If she had, what a wonder she might have made."

"What did she grow here?"

In response, Vitrine knelt where the greenhouse work-bench had been, where Chanda had used small match-sticks wrapped in scraps of wool to transfer pollen from one blossom to another, where she had slit the shells of long-dormant seeds to see if they might be encouraged to grow. She had been careful, so careful, but the most careful human in the world was never proof against the flick of a demon's finger.

Vitrine sought through fifty years of neglect, picking through the clay and the rock and the wood ash until she found what she was looking for: a double-lobed seed that slumbered in a shell too thick to easily pierce. With one sharp thumbnail, she split the purplish-black skin to reveal the white flesh inside. It released a quick green odor, and encouraged, she set it in the ground, covering it with her hand.

Chanda's name was written in her book, and so was what Chanda wanted to call this plant, before she remem-bered and broke every precious pane of glass and returned her success to the fire where it had come from. For Chanda, she could wait for a little while, some few months, perhaps even the full run of the year, to see if anything could be made of the seed she had dropped.

The angel did not move. Instead he paced the perimeter where the walls had fallen, bending down to pick up the fingers of the stone angel briefly before throwing them down again.

"What are you doing now?" he asked, and she shrugged.

"I am waiting."

"For?"

"For something to change."

She thought he might fly off then, too frustrated at her strangeness and the blasted barren quality of ground that had been three times scourged, but instead he knelt opposite her, placing his hand over hers. His hands were broad and squared, the nails pristine. They were entirely without lines or calluses, and she wondered for a moment what it would be like to cleave them joint from joint, cleaning them and separating the bones of his fingers. They would rattle like ivory dice on the broken pavers of Azril, or perhaps they would chime. She angrily jerked her eyes away to meet his.

"This isn't yours," she hissed, but he only shook his head.

"May the light forbid that it should be," he retorted, and under her hand and his, something happened.

It was a twitch, so small that it barely budged more than a few grains of soil, and then another, and another. She looked down at his hand, and she would have pulled away if it were not for what she was protecting underneath.

Another day passed, another day after that, and she drew a quick breath as something came up to tickle her palm, first shyly, and then more insistently, and then he pulled away, standing up, his face impassive. She gave him a haughty look and waited another day to show him that she had no regard for what he did or did not do.

When she did lift her hand, it was to reveal a tender pale sprout coming from the earth, the two tiny leaves curling like the horns of a ram.

"Oh *Chanda*," she said, full of the woman who had come from Johari with a half-dozen deaths on her head.

She watched, breath held, as a month passed, then another, and another. The plant was not meant to be a fast grower, but this one was, and she would have roared at the angel to quit with his tricks if her eyes hadn't been full of this new life, the thick straight stalk, the frilled leaves that looked too pale to be healthy.

"She would have had it far earlier, if only she could have borne for it not to be beautiful," Vitrine said without thinking, and the angel, who had never looked at the plant growing at all, frowned.

"Was it meant to be a beautiful plant?"

"A mother wants her child to have every advantage," Vitrine said, and then she remembered Avaline Demorsico and the crane that would never be her. She shut her mouth and refused to open it for another four months.

They waited together in the ruins of the greenhouse, the angel as properly upstanding as the statue had been, Vitrine perched on the pedestal, her feet swinging above the earth. When the rains came, she stretched a fold of sailcloth over her head like a courtesan with a fringed veil. The angel was too proud to heed the rain. He let it soak his clothes and run off his body as if he were a building, a guardhouse or perhaps some fine municipal thing clad in marble and glass. She would have liked him better if he was, but instead he was an angel, and sometimes she amused herself by shying rocks at his feet, at the broken walls behind him.

Between them, Chanda's plant ceased growing taller, but Vitrine could tell that it was still growing, the secret alchemy of its heart searching and waiting for what it needed to mature.

Come along, little one, Vitrine mouthed. *Come out. The world is so wide and wonderful, and it cannot do without you.*

On the third day after the rains stopped, when the sun shone like a new gold coin with the world for the buying, the first flowers appeared. They were tiny and crimson, the red of carmine rather than of blood, and they rolled out like tiny delicate tongues from a tight bud, spreading open to devour the world.

Vitrine touched the half-dozen flowers in wonder, and when she bent her head to kiss them, they trembled with some remembered fragment of Chanda's love of dark things and a bit of her fatal despair as well.

"No, no, be joyous," Vitrine whispered to them, her lips stinging with their polluted dew. "Be joyous, daughter of Chanda, and you will be a queen."

"Such promises you make," the angel muttered, and she would have been sharp with him if her eyes hadn't been full, if she couldn't hear the echo of a lost woman's laugh in her chest.

Vitrine and the angel waited as the moon waxed and waned and grew full again on the dreams of broken towers. The flowers fell and were in their turn replaced by lunar-white berries, tinged with a becoming blue.

When she saw them, Vitrine started to cry. Her tears splashed to the soil and amended it with a sorrow that leached through the roots and gave the plant an extra dose of deadliness that it would carry ever afterwards.

"Oh, that Chanda could see you," she whispered, stroking the leaves.

The angel, bored at the beginning of the rains and

impatient by the time the flowers withered, looked at the plant with his nose wrinkled in disgust and confusion.

"Another poison in the world," he declared finally, inspecting it from every angle. He had paced a track around Vitrine and the plant, round and even, but now he stood within the circle with them.

"Yes, angel?"

"Yes. Another wracken, another hellebore, another houndsdeath. You've only made another way for people to kill each other."

"Oh, no," Vitrine said sweetly. "*We* have made another way for people to kill each other. Chanda couldn't do it on her own, and it would have taken me longer without your steadying hand, without your strength. What shall we name our daughter?"

Once she had watched a pair of maids kill a guardsman behind a tavern, on him like two weasels with the knives they used to pare vegetables in the kitchen. Afterwards in their room, they gazed at each other with wonder at what they had made, both the torn body in the alley and the changes they had wrought in each other with such a thing between them. Everything was new, and one reached out to touch the other's parted lips.

The angel reared back with a fury, for an instant nothing more than a coil of light and a righteous rage older than the world. His sword—will and word and temper—flashed as quick as a snake bite over the plant, but then it froze as if he had driven it into the heart of a thousand-year pine tree.

Between his sword and the plant that would come to be known as devil's daughter, there was Vitrine, standing straight as a spear, her eyes a dare and her mouth a cruel joke.

"*Yes,* angel?" she asked, and she saw the defeat in his eyes even before he would admit it.

He vanished his sword, baring his teeth and mostly a man again except for the way the light clung to his hems like mud. He spat on the ground between them and turned, wings opening to grab the air and throw him towards the cliffs where once the anchoresses lived and cried. She watched him ascend until he was grown as small and insignificant as a sandhill crane or a dropped seed, and then she turned back to their creation.

"You will remake the world a time or two, my darling," she whispered, plucking up the lushest and most beautiful berry and popping it in her mouth. The taste of a thousand deaths stained her tongue, faithless husbands, vengeful daughters, kings and shepherds and librarians and duelists all coming to bow to their new conqueror.

It tasted very fine, and Vitrine smiled up at the darkening sky.

⚜

No one loves a city like one born to it, and no one loves a city like an immigrant. No one loves a city like they do when they are young, and no one loves a city like they do when they are old. The people loved the city of Azril in more ways than could be counted. Vitrine loved her city like demons and cats may love things, with an eye towards ownership and the threat of small mayhem.

Arvan Pilare, dark and gaunt with a neatly clipped beard and mustache, fastidious, distracted, and mostly silent, loved the city as it really was, which was to say he loved it as very few ever did.

"You know, I don't understand you," Vitrine said one early morning, sitting beside Arvan as he sketched the fishing ships leaving the harbor. Sometimes he thought she was a ragged man at the tavern near his apartment, and sometimes he thought she was a cockle seller who sometimes treated him to a paper packet of cockles steamed open and sprinkled with vinegar and horseradish. Today she was a knocker-up; the staff that she used to rap on windows and wake people for their morning shifts leaned by her side as she shared his perch on the walkway above the shore.

"What's to understand?" he asked, not looking up from his drawing. It was a bad habit, one that would have gotten him robbed five or six times over if a demon hadn't been curious about him and wanted to see how he turned out.

"You could make it more beautiful if you erased that one point off the rocks there," Vitrine said, gesturing. "See? Then it would match the one on the other side, so they would be balanced."

She had thought about doing just that. The spar of rock that aggravated her stood taller than most of the masts in the harbor, big enough she couldn't budge it on her own. She was waiting for one of her siblings to pass through who might have the strength to do so. She could take them out for a dinner of fried oysters, buy them some new clothes, and then ask them to knock off that peak that had been bothering her for some time now.

Arvan made a humming noise, not quite a laugh, not quite a sigh.

"Well, it wouldn't be real, then, would it? It wouldn't be as good as what I am drawing now."

"But it would be more beautiful," Vitrine insisted, and he drew in the shadows off the sail of the small fishing boat belonging to the Umars, who had been here much longer than Vitrine herself. There was some trouble there this generation, an eldest son who didn't want the family business, a younger daughter who did. Vitrine resolved to tend to that before it got too bad, but then Arvan spoke again.

"I don't want it to be beautiful if it isn't true," he said, and she snorted, flicking the paper with her nail.

"You're never going to sell anything," she said, and his only response was a peaceable *all right* that made her frown and leave. Let the robbers have him if he couldn't see sense.

She didn't think about him again until her sibling Passim came to visit her the next summer. They loved the oysters and they adored the indigo skirts and light girdles hung with silver charms that were so popular that year. The two of them ended the night in the snug study of the city's chief banker who slumbered all unknowing above, unaware that two demons were helping themselves to his sweetest wine and his strongest hashish.

They stretched out on the fine silk and wool rugs, turning the air blue with smoke, and they spoke of many things, which siblings they loved most, which they could not stand, and which they hated but also loved so much it was worse than simply hating them outright.

Finally, Passim turned their head to look at Vitrine, and

in the light from the many candles, it occurred to Vitrine that there was something sweet in Passim's wolf face, where the teeth were so long they couldn't properly close their mouth.

"Tell me, sister. You have been so kind. Is there anything I can do for you before I leave tomorrow? I should not like to see you struggle with anything too large when you are only so gentle."

It was on the tip of her tongue to say that Passim should knock the spar of rock off the harbor cliffs as they headed out to sea, but for some reason, she stopped herself.

"No, only remember to kiss Obla for me and to tell her that I miss her, that is all."

Vitrine saw Passim off the next day, and then she took on the seeming of a very wealthy woman from the mansions in the west. The old woman at Arvan's boarding-house squinted at her suspiciously, torn between fawning and spitting on her well-made shoes, but she called Arvan down and Vitrine whisked him away to a restaurant on Camellia Street. The waiter brought them a large platter of snails and a tiny cushion studded with silver needles to dig out the meat.

"I want you to do some work for me," Vitrine said. "I want you to capture this city, all of it."

Arvan blinked, twisting his needle delicately so that the flesh popped out of the snail shell in a complete spiral.

"But of course," he said cautiously. "I can do the spires and the harbors, and the great houses . . ."

"Well, of course you will do all of those. But I said I want all of it. I want the shops and the taverns. I want the starving children along the river and the courtesans in their beds. I want the faces of the men at the grain share markets, and the ships, every ship in the harbor, I want that."

Arvan considered her. He would come to know what she was, or at least he would have a better guess than almost anyone else would. That was probably when he started to suspect.

"That will be very expensive," he said, and she waved an impatient hand.

"Of course you will be paid. I shall pay you whatever you like."

Still he hesitated.

"My work is not always beautiful."

"Then make it true, and I will content myself with that."

She put a golden coin on the table between them, barely clipped, and then set down another two beside it.

"What does this get me?" she asked, and he stared.

"That's six months of my life on the table, you know."

Vitrine pouted, warming to her role as Lady Plenty. She passed her hand over the gold, and it doubled.

"There, a full year," she said, rising from the table in a swish of marigold skirts. "Meet me here in a year with what you have to show me. No paintings, I think, just drawings in ink. I suggest that when you come, you impress me."

"Or what?"

She showed him her teeth, white as any aristocrat's and sharper than a lion's.

"Or you will disappoint me," she said, and she left.

Single days could be very slow, but weeks passed very quickly. That year there was a new method for straightening wood that made for stronger ships, and someone discovered the bones of a magnificent dragon bedded in the cliffs down the coast. A team of clerics from Sui and faraway Tuyet arrived with delicate chisels and makeup brushes to painstakingly dig it out, and Vitrine went to join them, spending the high summer poring in fascination over the ancient past emerging from the stone. At night, she went to sit beside the dragon's jaws, still blackened with soot from the furnace of its belly.

"Who were you?" she marveled. "Who did you love?"

Sui claimed the bones of one foreclaw and Tuyet took the other. The rest was carefully transported to Azril where Vitrine had replacements for the missing parts carved from light wood and then gilded. The dragon posed magnificently in the city's hall of records, overseeing the deeds and contracts with its great empty eyes.

By then, Vitrine was almost late getting back to the restaurant to meet up with Arvan. He had ordered the snails again, but before they came, he passed her a leather folder filled with ink drawings.

She was silent as she flipped through them, nibbling on her lower lip as she took in her city in a new way, through the eyes and the skills of another.

Oh, it is rather dirty and shabby down by the river, isn't it? Perhaps I shall whisper to the mayor to put more money there.

"I do not know how I like these," she complained. "Azril is not at all flattered, and neither am I."

"It is too late to reclaim your money," Arvan started stiffly, and she waved him off.

"Of course it is. I do not particularly like these pictures, but you have given me exactly what I have asked for. Here."

She put down twelve gold coins.

"Two years?"

"No, just one. I'll see you again in a year."

"Ah. But . . . will you stay for snails?"

Vitrine blinked slowly, catlike.

"I think I shall."

She visited his new studio a few times the next year, lurking in the shadows as he turned his light sketches into completed ink drawings for her. This year, there were more portraits in the mix, some important, most not. Even Vitrine could not be everywhere at once, and she congratulated herself on buying his gaze for her own. She came to enjoy their yearly meetings, finding out what she had missed and what had caught his interest.

So it continued, but on the thirteenth year, there was only a note waiting for her at the appointed place: an apology and a request that she come to his residence, now a fine apartment close to Verdant.

She could smell the sickness immediately upon entering. When the solemn-faced boy servant escorted her to the bedroom, she pulled back the bedcurtains to reveal a rail-thin body with a bulging belly and a staring face yellowed with illness.

"I'm sorry," he said. "I have had better days."

"You have," she said, taking her seat by his side. "Show me my drawings."

There were fewer that year, but she studied them as avidly as she ever did. The scenes depicted were closer to his home, and then finally they were only what Arvan could see from his bed, the faces of his servants, the bowl of geraniums, his chamberpot, and the silver tray stacked with sticky dark pills for when the pain grew too great.

"These are excellent," Vitrine said finally. "It is not beautiful, but it is true."

She almost stood to go, but for the first time, Arvan took her hand.

"I have more drawings to make for you, far more. Can you keep me a while longer?" he asked, and she winced at the hope in his eyes.

"No." She wished she could. She had always wished she could.

He nodded, letting his hands fall from hers.

"After I've gone on, there is something that is yours held in trust with my men of business, Li and Staten on Law Street. It is yours no matter what, but I wonder if you will do me a favor."

"I like presents. What favor?"

"See the city for what it is as well as what you want it to be. Be . . . be kind, if you can."

Vitrine nodded. It was a rather big favor. Demons were not kind as a matter of course, but she could be kinder than not. There was a great deal of mischief in that balance, especially the sort she liked best.

He breathed his painful last three weeks later, and in widow's black, Vitrine went to see Li and Staten on Law Street, who handed her a fat leather folder. They told her it had been added to frequently, starting with just a few sheets and then, in the last years, the additions coming in a flurry.

She took the folder and went to sit on the roof of Arvan's house to inspect it. Below her, his servant boy wept over him, and she absently promised him another love if he would only be quiet. He agreed without realizing he had, and now she was able to open the folder.

Inside, it was her.

The pages of her book fluttered in wonder at the shock, that she had been seen and seen so often. It looked like he had only managed it by accident a few times in the first year, catching glimpses of her among the dragon dig crews and in the hurried rushing at the flower market. As the years went on, he developed the trick of finding her in the most unlikely places, chattering with the women at the pumps, napping among the colony of cats at Dise, dancing the ganli for the death of the last Lord Mayor.

By the last few years, she suspected he was seeking her out. Over and over again, he found her, and he put her in the city, not beautiful, but true, as true a thing as there ever was, the demon of Azril.

Her tears ran down her face to splash on the page, where she argued with a fishseller over the price of sturgeon, and it was only then she realized that she had no picture of Arvan himself. There were the dockmen, the goldsmiths, the courtesans, the beggars, the sick and the well, the vicious and the gentle, the loved and those lost, but Arvan wasn't there, and she wept harder.

Finally, she pulled out her book, and pressing so hard she dented the page and the one underneath it, she wrote his name. Suddenly she wished she could draw too, but that was never one of her talents and she closed her book again.

EIGHT

Two summers later and Vitrine had cleared out the streets. At first she had taken what was left of her dearly departed to the valleys beyond the city, hauling them in a handcart and then in a wagon pulled by a feral horse she had broken for the purpose. The horse was a stout bay with the noble head of a conqueror's mount and the short and blocky body of a butcher's pony. After she had tamed some of the willfulness out of him and seduced him with the promise of the wild rice that had started to grow in the high rivers again, they got on quite well as he pulled his burden of dead people to the valleys.

Cartload by cartload Vitrine thought she was making a dent, but then came the day when she went down an alley she scarcely remembered off Tintagel Street. The remnants of the dead, the bones, the metal of their belt buckles and their swords and their jewelry, so *much,* and all tossed among the rubble. She picked up one of the iridescent beetles crawling on a half-buried skull and squashed it angrily between her fingers before flicking it away with just the softest ripple of guilt.

The horse butted his heavy oversize head against her shoulder, and she pushed him away so hard he nearly went down on his hocks. Then she simply sat for a while in the silent street, tracing her fingertips along the nearly intact rib cage of a girl whose flute music she could still hear in her head.

In just an hour or so, she was back on her feet, lifting her chin angrily. Where she lacked resolve and peace, anger would do, and she unhitched the horse from the wagon.

"The wild rice can be found north along the river," she told him. "The shoots are small and green and tender now. You can go find them and eat until you explode for all of me."

With the horse fled, she took her spade and piled more rocks over the fallen.

I'm really just rearranging them, she thought before she pushed it down.

Buried was buried, and if she troubled herself about it too much, she would freeze and only be fit for reforming the city a single paver at a time. They could lie where they had fallen, and they could sleep under the new streets.

She had covered half the dead with rubble—why were there so many? Had they crammed into the small space thinking it might protect them? Was there some other disaster that had found them before the angels did?—when the angel came walking down the cleared street, the bay trotting chastened and docile by his side.

"I found this one heading for the high ground," he said, offering her the lead. "He would have joined one of the herds if I had not stopped him."

Vitrine wiped the sweat from her brow, giving him a weary look.

"So?"

The angel looked at her work, the burying of the dead where they had fallen, and wordlessly released the horse a second time. The horse whickered as if fed up with the whole mess and took to his heels, and Vitrine went back to her spade and the patch of ground directly in front of her. If she could just clear that single patch of ground, she would be all right. There would be another and another afterwards, but eventually, there would be no more and she could stop.

"You are turning your city into a graveyard," the angel observed.

"No, you did that," she retorted. "*You* brought the judgment. *You* brought the fire. *You* listened to no testimony and heard no cries. You."

"I could say that you were the one who made this city into what it was."

She turned a perfect mezavolta, spinning on the ball of her foot in a swirl of sailcloth skirts, but instead of blowing a kiss to the angel as she would have to her partner in the dance, she threw a shovelful of corpse dirt at him instead. The humus hit him on the chest with a damp thud and stained the linen of his robes in a deeply satisfying way.

He made a disgusted sound, falling back, and then he drew himself up again icily.

"You throw dirt like a child. Or a pig."

"Is there a difference to you?" she asked, turning back to her work. "You roasted them both alike."

He watched her work as the sun set and rose and set, and an hour before dawn, when she paused to mark the passage of a comet that had passed through Azril's skies only a dozen times since she had claimed the city for her own, he finally spoke again.

"You could divert the river through the streets," he offered. "A hundred-year flood would carry this all away, leave it clean."

"And scatter them," she said wearily. "And leave a generation of patchwork ghosts to roam the floodplain. And I would never know where they had gone."

"You don't remember all of them," the angel protested. "You can't."

In response, she bent and lifted up a cracked pelvis, stained orange from the rust of the belt buckle that rested upon it.

"Petyr Morozin," she said. "Three generations of Azril, first of his family to enter the priesthood. He was a good priest, and so of little interest to me. He fed people who were hungry, he encouraged the good, and when he could not stamp out the bad, he restrained it as best he knew how. He liked his wine, but I certainly won't hold it against him at this late date."

She set the pelvis respectfully back on the ground and picked up a femur.

"Lillith El-Adular. Actress who admitted no past but whichever one she made up. Motherless, fatherless, childless, loved by everyone who saw her and untouched. The world slipped off of her like she was made of glass, and it only loved her the better for it."

The skull she picked up next was missing half the teeth in its jaw.

"I remember when this one still had all her teeth. They

gleamed in her mouth until a shying horse knocked them out, and then she had false ones carved for her from the tusk of a sea cow. Her jaw pained her for the rest of her life, the echo of that kick sounding in her dreams, but Huyen Lang was still one of the best drovers in the city, still led the wagons from the docks up to the stations in the west."

She set down the skull to pick up another, crying out when the angel seized her by the wrist, causing the skull to strike the ground and shatter.

She reached down for the bone shards that scattered whitely at her feet, but he would not let her bend, instead keeping her on her feet. With a cat's hiss, she clawed at his fingers, and when she went for his eyes, he took that hand too, holding her still.

"Stop it. They are dead as we will never be. Leave them here. Let them rest."

"Like I should leave you? Do you believe that if I forget my city and all the people who made it my city that I would let you go?"

His fingers tightened painfully on her wrists, a warning perhaps, but what use were warnings when the worst had already happened?

"Oh, you do think that, don't you?" she murmured. "If I left Azril, perhaps I would leave you as well. Or at least, I would pluck out that piece of myself that you bear with such tedious patience."

"Not so patient."

Her lips parted over her teeth, something that was once a smile.

"Show me."

He let her go abruptly, shying back like the bay might have done, but he didn't flee. The bay could go upriver, beyond her grasp, and the angel couldn't. Instead, she watched fascinated as his hand ghosted up towards his chest and dropped again hastily.

"Show me," she repeated, and with a soft, pained exhale, he lifted his shirt up to his throat, showing her the mass of scarring over his heart. It was an unnatural wound on impossibly perfect flesh, her curse given form. It made her stare, and without thinking, she came closer. She hadn't done it, but she had caused it, and she pressed the ball of her thumb to the marks that rutted his flesh like a plow over the earth.

"You scar," she said with something like wonder.

"I shouldn't. I."

Vitrine wondered vaguely what he had intended to say. She didn't much care because it wasn't true. Once you wounded a thing, it scarred if it didn't die first. Perhaps he was the first of his brothers to have ever been wounded; it wasn't impossible. Once you were wounded, if you were lucky, you scarred. He was lucky without being grateful for it, and she laid her hand over his marks, just barely covering them with her palm.

Under her touch, his breathing went shallow.

"This is all of you I care to touch. Just this part."

"The ruined part."

"The part that's mine."

She stepped back as if it meant nothing to her.

"You wear it well."

"I don't."

It came out almost plaintive, and she went back to

shoveling the bones underneath the dirt while he hovered close and then fell behind her.

It took another two weeks before she declared herself done, and as she washed her feet in a fountain filled with clean rain, it occurred to her that she had spoken to the angel in anger and not in grief. It was a thin difference, grieved anger and not angry grief, but it felt like an important one, and she nodded, pleased.

The rain washed away the clouds, leaving the sky a polished bronze platter, and far above, she could see the shape of the angel, wings wider than even an eagle's or an albatross's.

Or a crane's, she thought, remembering the taste of the crane girl's flesh in her mouth.

Vitrine wondered if he pretended that Azril's broken towers were the peerless spires of his home. She wondered if it pained him to be apart from it, from his brothers and his work.

She did not wonder what was in his heart, because she knew, and as the sky shifted gold to lazuli, she smiled.

NINE

The rains came, and this year, they brought with them a cold that sank into Vitrine's bones. She had come from much warmer places, where the rain was a blessing because it took over the world completely and deeply and only for a handful of days. In those lands, the rains came down as if they loved the land, and the land opened to take them, greedily draining the water until the cereus and the jade plants burst into bloom, unable to help themselves.

The rains of Azril were heavy and soaking, turning her hair and her clothes into weights that might drown her, and so she went up into the anchoresses' cells that bit into the high cliffs.

The rope ladders and pulley systems would have rotted away by now even without the work of the angels, so Vitrine scaled the cliff like a spider, her fingers finding holds in the sheer rock.

The lower cells were large and spacious, chipped away by decades of women who had found their place easily and swiftly. Vitrine ignored them, climbing to the narrow uppermost cells, the ones that sometimes had to be entered with a stooped back, or, if the anchoress in question was very tall, perhaps on her knees. The upper cells were bare of the comforts offered closer to the ground. They dug deep into the cliff, long eyebolt tunnels that would open to an animal-like burrow at the end.

Vitrine crawled to the very rear of the cell she chose and still she could hear the rain pelting down, swelling the river by increments, drowning the streets. If Azril was as it had been, it would be full of people, unhappy to be out, unhappy to be kept in, selling all manner of physics and remedies for the aches the turn of the weather brought on. There would be children playing in the overflowing fountains, risking their lives by swimming in the sea, catching golden fish that might grant them wishes and falling in love with the mermaids who occasionally washed up after the storms.

In the darkness, Vitrine pulled out her book, the first time she had touched it in a long while. It felt strange in her hands, almost revolting. It felt like holding a dead person, and in a way, she was. She was holding thousands of dead people, and the mellow softness of their rotting bodies and the spar-sharpness of their bones turned her stomach.

Then she remembered that even if it was rotten, it was hers, and she hugged the book to her chest, her shoulders heaving in a heavy sob and then another.

She cried like the rain did, relentlessly and without fury, just the idiot fall of water that slid down her cheeks as if she were as indifferent as rock.

One of her siblings, short, fat, almost rectangular with hands like cenotaphs, lived in the heart of a mountain, and long ago, they had filled the tunnel in after themself. They were the warm heart at the center of the stone, and when Vitrine lay down on the slope and pushed her ear to the rock, she could detect a sweet and constant thrum, their joy and content passed through silica and shale.

That could be me, Vitrine thought, hugging her book tighter. *I would be the heart of the mountain and I would pull it closed after me. Perhaps when I woke up, the wheel of time would grow bored of rolling forward and instead it would roll back. I would walk backwards down the slope and find my Azril just as it was.*

She closed her eyes tight and tried to believe her own lies, but belief would not come, and neither would sleep. Instead she only cried, and when she grew too cold, she tore a page out of her book and lit it with a puff of her breath. It was as dry as good tinder, and it lit up immediately, a bright flare with a blue lip at the base. Vitrine caught a glimpse of what she had written on the page—a recipe from Noor for goose stuffed with spiced fried barley, olives, and raisins—and then it was gone.

She tasted the savory greasiness of the goose, sharpened by the brined olives and then softened by the plump raisins—and then it was gone. Less one page, her book was lighter, and she reached for another one. When she tore it out, she saw it was a list of songs sung in the galleries of the western mansions. It tickled her that the tunes played by the serious young heirs to the city were lifted up from the genius of one man who worked the brothels and the stews, singing his clever songs to draw in the patrons with money. He was no lyricist, constantly rhyming *bandy* with *randy,* but his tunes were haunting, ghosts from another time, the past or a future that was too bright to even dream of. Those she had stolen and set to poetry from a twenty-years-dead girl who had churned them out by the yard for lovers with passion and money but no rhyming talent.

The paper went up, and Vitrine almost moaned at how warm it was. For just an instant, she felt as light as the ash that coated her fingers, light enough to reach for a third page and then a fourth.

Her book was large and heavy. She had many pages to go through, but it would never have lasted forever. It might not even have lasted the day, but the angel spoke up from the mouth of the tunnel.

"What are you doing in there?" he asked.

She scowled, the ashes of a family of apothecaries who specialized in mixing ink floating down around her. They had come originally from Padri with a recipe for a thin springtime green stolen from the guild there. With the seafarers and thieves of Azril just beyond their doorstep, they had developed a gorgeous and extraordinarily pricey peacock blue, a bold fuchsia that smelled like roses, and a green based off their stolen darling that stung the fingers in wordless reprimand when someone wrote lies. Their page was bright with lapis and orpiment and cinnabar, and when it burned, it filled the cell with caustic smoke.

"What do you care what I'm doing?" she asked, and then she wished that she had said something that made her sound a little less like a petulant child.

"I love you," he said impatiently. "Of course I want to know what you are doing."

His blunt words surprised a laugh out of Vitrine, hiccupping and sharp in her chest after the tears. It tasted of chemical ash, but it was still a laugh, and she shook her head.

"Oh, by all the mansions beneath the earth and all the clever ones who live in them," she said. "You are ridiculous."

"If I am ridiculous, it is only because you have made me so," he said.

There was a deliberate scrape of a sandal on the rock, a concession for her, she knew. He could be as silent as she was, and she considered this small courtesy as he approached.

He is tall enough he has to stoop, she thought idly. *If I had my sister Oroba's sword, I could cut his head off.*

She had no sword, and even if she did, she was suddenly afraid that she was too cold to wield it. It had nothing to do with her stiff fingers or the aching muscles that locked in the chill. It was something deeper that told her that perhaps she could bear it best if she was only still, only stone. She thought she might do anything to be truly warm again.

The angel emerged into the chamber just as the next page, dedicated wholly to a remarkable person who had shown themself at the sideshow and turned the money from that into a mansion, burnt to the end. At the last, the flame leaped up ruddy gold like Sophronia's hair had been, and extinguished with a resentful hiss. Vitrine caught a glimpse of the angel's face, and then the eradicating dark put them both out. Neither of them might have been there at all, and Vitrine thought about where else they might be instead. Perhaps she would still be on the low dry fields, cursing the bulls to attack one another so that their blood fell to the ground and grew soldiers. Perhaps the angel would be with his own kind, someplace empty, someplace clean.

Instead they were here inside the mountain, and after a

moment, she heard him come to sit down before her. In the dark, Vitrine suspected he looked less like a man, more like what he had been before there were things to speak with and commands to be issued. Without her eyes to interfere, he felt like a gathering storm.

She started to tear another page from her book, but his hand came out to grasp hers. It was gentle, but she jerked her hand back as if he had clawed her, clapping her book shut and clutching it to her chest.

"You should not burn your book."

"It's mine. I may do what I like with it."

He snorted.

"Even children know not to break their own toys."

"You have not known many children, and it is not a toy."

She slid it back into the glass cabinet in her heart, and immediately a tide of relief swelled over her. Safe, as safe as she could make anything, and she sat for a moment with her arms wrapped around her body, clutching herself tight. It was warmer with her book inside her rather than set on fire, and she stared through the darkness to where the angel sat.

"I know you like destroying things very well. Why would you stop me?"

"I wouldn't destroy something that was mine," he said with a scornful note in his voice.

"Then what is yours?"

A long silence. The darkness shifted in front of her, perhaps as if he were shaking his head, perhaps as if his hands twisted together restlessly in his lap.

"Properly, nothing. We are forbidden gifts or payment. What we have, we have from the start."

"Except you."

She reached for him, and without sight, she touched his shoulder, slid her fingers down to the left side of his chest. Vitrine considered, and then she dug her taloned fingers into the scarring over his heart, seeking the flesh to rip it open. The angel grunted with pain, one hand coming up to wrap around her wrist, but he didn't stop her. She tolerated the grasp of his fingers to feel the way they trembled, and she did not withdraw her claws from his skin until his blood soaked into the fibers of his shirt, mingling with the rain, plastering it to his body.

He held on when she pulled back, only releasing her when she shook him off, and the sound he made, angry and exalted—she could feel it in his blood, that part of him that needed her—went straight to her core. It could crack glass, it could spill ink, and she leaned back against the rock wall.

"Go. Leave."

She heard the angel sigh like the sound of a wind rushing down a narrow valley. There was no other sound, but there was suddenly more space around her, more air to breathe.

She slept for a while, and when she woke up, the air was drier, and she could no longer hear the rains outside. Vitrine realized that she had slept them out, and perhaps that was a mercy.

She made her way out of the tunnel, and she yelped when she almost tripped over the angel, who was sitting on the ledge. He turned to look at her, his face solemn.

"You are awake. I thought you might wait out the year."

"I still might," she said stubbornly. "Why are you still here?"

"You know the answer to that."

He no longer sounded angry about it, which disturbed her in a way that she couldn't quite define. He was tired, it was written in every line of his face. He was impatient, as she could tell from the hoarse catch in his voice. He was lonely, which she had not guessed angels might be when they were apart from their own kind. He was not angry, and she scowled.

"You deserve it. You should not have destroyed my city."

Instead of responding, he turned towards the ruins again.

"You have a great deal of work to do. What comes next?"

He reminded her that once, one of the noble families had caused to be built a colonnade where each of the supporting pillars was an angel carved from marble. They were not real angels, of course, only even-featured, blank-eyed men and women in draping robes carrying the weight of the entablature on their noble heads. Real angels came like a storm, like a nightmare, like the end of the world, and he looked a little less like them now, a little more like a patient stone statue that bore the firmament on his head.

"You don't look much like an angel anymore," she said, refusing to give him the pleasure of knowing how he resembled something she had once loved in Azril.

"I *am* an angel. That is exactly what I look like. And I ask you. What comes next?"

There was a part of her that wanted to tell him to rot in the anchoress cells. Enough women had, the ones who were imprisoned in the cliffs rather than choosing them willingly. Sometimes the lower cells flooded towards the rear, filling with silted water that rotted the skin off their feet.

Instead, she looked down at the city, her work barely a

dent in what would need to be done, and then she looked back at the angel, a storm, a disaster, pure and noble power shaped to look like a handsome man.

"Next, I go home."

Wordlessly, he followed her down the cliff, his wings spread like a sheltering shadow over her as she descended in the form of a black kite.

TEN

It distressed Vitrine how much of the city had to come down. A good lot of it already had in the years she had been burying and restoring, but Azril, thanks to its love of fire and the scouring waves from the sea, had always preferred to build with stone rather than with wood.

Much of the stone they used, cut from quarries that filled with acidic water when it rained, was proof against common flame and salt, but in the scourge of the angels, it grew porous and soft, crumbling and chalky, powdering the pads of Vitrine's fingers when she pushed too hard. The older stone, granite that had come from some older city that came before, that would stay, proof against everything that had come before, but the newer stone was fragile and untrustworthy.

"Not fit to build with," she said to herself. The angel stood at her shoulder and a little behind, for all the world like a diligent foreman taking his orders. She spoke to him because otherwise she had no one to speak to but the cranes and the deer that sometimes wandered down from the hills, and sometimes, she thought that he might even have been listening.

"When they come back, they'll need places to live, and so much of this, it's a ruined tomb, isn't it? They can't squat in here like grave ghouls. They can't live under buildings that might just drop on their heads if they sneeze . . ."

She walked the city back and forth, shaking her head as one building after another proved unsound. There were some buildings that stood almost as proud and beautiful as they had before, missing only a roof or a wing. Seen from an angle and close enough to block out the rest of the neighborhood, she could pretend it was only a quiet day, and any minute, people would come out or rush in on important business. However, even they were pitted and fragile, as apt to fall as to shelter, and she knew that one way or another, they had to be taken care of.

The angel watched as she unearthed a forge and a casket of iron ingots, his head tilted slightly.

"You need fire," he observed.

"I can't bring down the rotten stone with a wood spade, so I'll make one from iron," she said. "Yes, I need fire."

The words were no sooner out of her mouth than she found herself in the angel's arms, held as snugly and securely as if she were a cat he was rescuing from danger. The ingots dropped out of her hands, clattering against the anvil, and then they were high above the city, looking down at it.

Vitrine yelped with surprise, and then she saw all the city below her as she had not the last time he lifted her. She saw the grid of streets and the towers, all broken but some still tall.

If I don't look at it straight on, if I do not look too closely, it's still there, she thought in wonder, and then the angel spoke.

A tremor shook the earth, so powerful that it struck them in the air as well, and then something deep below the city groaned as if it was hungry, and rose up, as if it had briefly been freed.

A dark cloud rose up from Azril—*the ghosts,* Vitrine thought for one wild moment, *the ghosts are leaving*—and then she saw that it was only the birds, all of them that could fly abandoning the young ones who couldn't, and the ground heaved up and something screamed across her mind, and then the buildings fell. The ruins turned to rubble, the stones cast like white bones onto the shore.

Out at sea, the waves churned up and pulled back from the shore, leaving the wrecks naked for a split second before rushing back and pounding flat what was left of the low town by the water, and Vitrine screamed so loudly that the earth went still and the angel dropped her.

She closed her eyes as she fell, her skirts fluttering up to make a sound like helpless, useless wings.

She looked up where she saw the angel hovering over her and over Azril with a silence that looked as much like judgment as it was surprise, and then she closed her eyes tightly. What was there to see after all? Nothing she could bear, nothing that would heal her or that was worth writing in her tattered book.

Vitrine hit the ground like a star, sending up a wave of dust and grime, sinking into what had been Murrine Square before the angels came. It was where the glass-blowers had set up their outdoor stands, puffing out globes of red and green and yellow for perfume bottles, witch's balls, and amphitres of poison. Sunk a good few feet below the surface of the street, Vitrine could smell decades of copper for blue and garnet-gold for ruby, almost the same as it was before.

With her eyes closed, Vitrine could sense more clearly what the angel truly was as he came down to land beside her. Her eyes told her he was a man, and without them to fool the rest of her, she could feel the way the heat of him wanted to singe her skin, how he smelled of something cold that lived between the stars, and how, barely audible, something of the song of creation hung over him.

"Are you hurt?" he asked anxiously.

"Of course. What a stupid question."

"Here, let me—"

She opened her eyes to see him reaching for her, and she bared her teeth, sharp enough to tear a strip of flesh off a crocodile.

"No!"

For a wonder, for a miracle, for a mercy, he stopped, doubt on his face and disapproval in his eyes.

"You cannot simply lie there—"

"I will if I wish to," she snapped. "You put me here."

"I didn't—I did what you wanted!"

"Then leave," she said, surprising them both.

They examined the two words she had thrown between them.

"And where shall I go?" he asked, his tone formal.

"Anywhere. I don't care."

"And what shall I do?"

"I told you to go fuck yourself once—"

"Several times."

"—and that still stands. I don't *care*."

He stood with his head bowed and his hands clasped in front of him. It wasn't penance—she didn't think that he was actually capable of such a thing—but it might have been humility.

"When may I return?" he asked softly.

There was something gnawing her, something as cruel as he could be, that gleefully wanted to tell him *never*. He could never come back. He could live with the contagion she had put inside him forever, let it eat him until it and his suffering and longing for home turned him into one of the leviathan, great and terrible bodies hidden under the mountains and the sea because they could not bear the earth and they were grown too heavy to seek the sky.

Something kept her from it, and she ignored whatever it was in favor of enjoying the thin thread of fear in his voice.

"Fifty years," she said. "Come back in fifty years."

The angel's shoulders slumped, he nodded, and a moment later he was gone. He could cross the world with a thought, find a single grain of gold in the desert sands. He could be anywhere and doing anything, and the only place he would not go was Azril.

When Vitrine could feel no hint of him in the air or the soil or the stone, she rose from her crater, and looked around.

The earthquake had shaken the lesser buildings to the ground. Everywhere there was dust, and where the stone had snapped instead of burst, it left a raw break, shiny and slick like the stone had been when it was fresh cut. There was something painfully new about the sight of it, but after the first flinch, Vitrine grew used to it. There would be newly cut stone again someday, and the buildings still standing, made of granite, made of basalt, stayed. They had been there before she arrived, and someday they would house new generations.

But only if I get to work, she thought.

ELEVEN

About twelve years after the angel departed, Vitrine came down from adjusting the flow of the river to find people on the beach. She was so startled to hear human voices again that she shied back into the darkness and shrouded herself in shadows, her blood racing and her eyes wide.

They had built a great bonfire on the sand to hold back the night, but she crept closer and closer yet, unblinking and fascinated. Had the first people of her Azril been like this? Had they built fires from the wood that washed up high on the shore, and had they roasted seabirds in the embers of their fire? Had they gestured with broad hands at what had been theirs and pointed to the mountains at what might be theirs again?

With the pleasure of an eavesdropper who knows she will not be caught, Vitrine came to sit at the fire, one more face the men were sure they knew, though if they counted, they would find themselves one more than they had been.

"It was an earthquake that brought down great Azril," one of the sailors said. "It opened the ground like a woman's legs, and what came out must surely fall back in."

"Pah," snorted another man. "We see what you know of women. No, it was fire, fire started from the toppled candle of a woman in the pleasure quarters. I know this because I knew a man who sailed with one who survived it. He said that it was a courtesan's candle, and from there raced the doom of the city."

"That's a story about disease, didn't you know? No, Azril fell because the Lord Mayor ordered it. He was in the pay of the Ithars, the horse people. When they gave him the weight of a princess in gold and threw in the princess besides, he opened the gates to let them in, and they leveled it. Time and fate did the rest."

"Azril fell because angels came from the east and set it afire," Vitrine said quietly, and suddenly every eye was on her.

She stared at the fire, which sent plumes of writhing smoke into the sky, and she was aware of the men around her surreptitiously reaching for the knives they had concealed in their clothing and the amulets they wore to ward off demons and bad dreams. She was both, and she was not offended.

"You are not welcome to our fire," the oldest man among them said finally. "You will not poison our food or taint our water. You will strike no man with blindness or ride his back home to turn his children into rats."

"Children into rats, I remember that one. You must be from the Iray River valley, where they sang of Bavion and Horu for so many years."

"Indeed we are. You are not welcome at our fire, you will not—"

"I am not, and I will not," she said. "Only get your story straight. Azril was struck down by angels."

The men sat quietly, respectfully, and Vitrine was almost

ready to rise and fade into the darkness again, nothing more than a story that they would tell others when they returned safely home, when one of the other men spoke up.

"What had Azril done to deserve that fate?"

In an instant, the fire was doused and the beach plunged into darkness. They were men of the Iray River valley, and so they knew the old stories. They did not run, and they did not cry out, but instead they sat still, as still as baby rabbits when the hawk's shadow appeared.

"Azril was set afire because angels opened their obedient mouths and spoke," she said, her lips inches from each man's ear. She was sorry when they did not flinch back from her, when they did not unthinkingly reach back and try to strike her. Then she would have been within her rights to rend them open through the middle, to reach through them and throw what made them living men instead of dead men into the still-steaming coals.

They sat like statues, and for the long hours of the night, she slid from one to the other, the thing in the darkness, the thing with claws, and she sat on their backs and hovered over their heads.

"Azril was set to fire by angels who came from the east. Azril fell because the angels spoke," she insisted, and no one was foolish enough to ask her again what sin deserved her crumbled towers and the silence after the festival.

She picked through their minds as the stars spun overhead, the Carriage carrying the Weaving Girl chased by the Demon who loved her. There were one or two men with cracks inside them enough that she could lever them wide if she wished, opening up chasms into which whole families could fall.

Vitrine toyed with the idea, let them feel the whisper of her passage and the depth of their own frailty, and then she let it go. It was enough that they knew, and so long as they remembered that Azril fell because the angels spoke, they could continue as cracked men instead of broken ones.

Finally, the sun slipped a gleaming edge over the horizon, and the hold she had on them broke. She slid into a shadow of driftwood, and the men, casting many glances behind them towards Azril, hurriedly packed to return to their ship.

"Wait," she said, looking at them from the top of a dune, and with dread scored on their faces, they turned to her.

They will not forget that night in a hurry, she thought with satisfaction. *They will not forget me so soon, even if I am not Horu or Bavion.*

"Leave your clothes on the beach," she said, and though they looked back and forth between each other, they stripped to the skin and set off again for their ship.

This time, she let them go, and when the striped sail disappeared over the horizon, Vitrine went down to the beach to pick through the piles of discarded garments.

The clothes were rough, of course, wool and linen rather than the silk that had once flowed into Azril like a shining road, but they had been gaily dyed with madder and woad and barberry, set with salt and iron whose savor she could still taste in the threads.

Since the fall of the city, she had gone around in rags when she even thought of it, and in the long days of burying the dead and clearing out the stone, her skin served to cover her as well as anything else.

Now she walked among the pile of clothes as if she were

at Folade's on Weave Street, with the smart girls bringing
her a dish of pink sugar with her tea and a dozen grades of
silk at her fingertips. Folade's had closed well before Azril
went up in flames, Vitrine recalled. Folade had had designs
on dressing the Lord Mayor's family, exclusively and in
perpetuity, but her head was turned by an immortal mercenary from Phyrros. The mercenary sailed east with a sail
patched with silk and the most talented dressmaker on the
continent beside her, not to mention a king's ransom of silk
in the hold, and that had been that.

*She will be venerable in her tomb now, if she did not meet
with some accident before,* Vitrine thought. *I wonder if she
had children to carry on her trade, if they were half so clever
as she was, as ambitious and as skilled.*

She had decided that the Mercers, the ones who left,
weren't hers, and they weren't. She paused, however, thinking of the children of Folade. Folade always wanted children,
if not from her own body than of her heart and her wits. It
was tempting, seductive even, to imagine one of those children in a workroom on what might someday be Weave Street
again, their head bent over a cutting table as their dressmaker's shears snipped through wool and silk, a tape measure
dyed in cochineal thrown carelessly around their neck.

*Folade will never return, but perhaps her grandchildren
might,* Vitrine thought, and a queer shiver ran down her
spine. Instead of looking back at the broken city behind
her, she looked out over the sea as well, a sailor's wide orange
sash clutched in her hands.

Where had Folade and her mercenary gone? Vitrine's
throat suddenly closed with an almost hundred-year worry
about whether that mercenary had taken good care of her,

if she was as careful with her mortal dressmaker as she wouldn't be of her own nearly indestructible body.

Immortal or not, I will tear her into bits so small that not even Folade's ghost will be able to stitch her back together if she hurt her.

Folade had left so quickly, even for a demon who reckoned a generation a small enough amount of time to spend enjoying a holiday by the river. Phyrros, likely, and then perhaps on to Muying? To the wet paving stones of Brid or the ever-burning towers of Binh Hoa? Who knew?

Vitrine glanced back at the city behind her, the stab of pain inevitable, but rueful frustration coming to live with it as well.

No fine patrons for their skills, no litters or carriages, no streets, no lights, and no one to dress.

She put on a large ocher shirt and a pair of indigo trousers spangled with white rings from where the fabric had been tied tight before dyeing. The orange sash, the best of the lot even to her inexpert fingers, she wrapped around her waist tightly, letting the fringed end hang down to her knees.

Vitrine turned to the horizon where Folade and her mercenary had gone.

"Come back," she said. "Please. Come home."

Newly dressed, she walked back to the fallen buildings to make sure they had a home to come back to.

TWELVE

Vitrine first came to the city clinging to a dream of heavy-headed red flowers bleeding their sedative scent into the air. She remembered roots and leaves, trowels and garden knives and eyes keen for any sign of white rot or mites. She wanted to love her city like a gardener loved her garden, with work, with occasional curses, with puzzle-solving and strange fixes, and finally with wonder for what lifted its head up to the sun.

That was the dream, and it was a good one, but the experience was a little more like walking through the bazaars in her lost city in the south, not the grand markets, but the lesser street affairs, where every year the households brought out their old things, their dented tea-urns, their dead grandparents' canes, their children's outgrown clothes and their books of outdated poetry. You would mostly find junk there, though often it was junk that looked better than your own junk, but once in a while, you could also find treasures.

Vitrine rifled through the dreaming minds of her new home and found in an overly grand house on Clayborn Street the only daughter of a retired pirate king. When she was younger, she had played pirate herself in her father's old salt-cracked coats in between lessons from tutors from all over the continent. Her father had stolen her from her mother on the Adani Islands, and that hurt, buried under a dozen years of good food and sweet tea and meticulous care, was still there, was just the kind of opportunity that Vitrine liked best.

She came to the pirate princess on moonlight and prised her fingers into the crack that neglect and brutal hurt had made. Vitrine smoothed the princess's black and coiled hair back from her ear and whispered to her of many things. She nurtured the discontent and nursed the ambition. She winnowed out cowardice and guilt like weeds, and when the princess was ready, she told her of a certain key that her father left in the mouth of a gargoyle on their roof.

One slick and rainy night, while her father was seeing to his ships on the floating pier, the princess braved the widow's walk in her bare feet, an old leather coat over her shift. When she reached into the gargoyle's fanged and smiling mouth, she found the key that she somehow knew was there.

The key opened a box under her father's bed, and she found within it a book bound in old boards and filled from beginning to end with the sins of the great and the powerful. The princess read her father's book all night as the rain pattered for entry at her shutters, and over her shoulder Vitrine read as well.

The pirate king's words were blunt and unsparing, and what he had done was written as clear as anything else. He had come to Azril with his fleet, turned them from sea raiders into an informal navy, and then, when things grew easy, into traders who never quite lost their taste for blood. He ruled the city like he had ruled his ships, with gold and kind words when they served, with knives and cunning when they would not, and it was all written down in his blocky script. The princess found her own mother in the pages, her fate finally clear after so long, and Vitrine rubbed soft soothing circles into the girl's back as she lay silently with her face in her clean linen pillows.

"You could put the book back," she murmured, her breath like the steam rising up from the kettle. "He won't ever know that it was gone. He would still be your father. You could still be his daughter. You could choose for it all to stay the same."

In truth, it was the last thing that Vitrine wanted. She could see the courage and viciousness in the princess like a splash of red in a line of white flowers, and she wanted it for her city. Still, she was clever enough not to build with weak timber, and she whispered excuses into the princess's ear, love and comfort and the beauty of a life that continued as sweetly as it always had.

"He loves you," Vitrine whispered, "and you love him. That is as true as the rest, isn't it?"

Vitrine thought that that would be the end of it. Love so often was.

However, when the princess rose up from the bed, she was different from the raw girl who had lain down, and her mouth was set in a line that would be the despair of her comportment teacher. *You cannot be pretty and hard,* the teacher from Combes said over and over again, but the princess lost in a heartbeat any use for *pretty*.

"He loves me. He threw my mother to the sharks. These things are both true," said the princess to the shadow in her room. In her memories, she would remember speaking to herself, to her mirror perhaps, or to the dress form where the silk gown for her seventeenth birthday celebration hung. She would not remember the shadow that drifted closer with a breath of pleasure and satisfaction, or the question it offered her.

"And what else is true?" asked the shadow, a little breathless.

"That he will regret both of these things."

When the pirate king died on his daughter's next birthday, his blood pooling around his head like some dark saint's halo and the servants already moving to take his corpse away, it was not regret that he felt, but surprise and aggravation.

"Did I not love her?" he asked the demon, as the laundress sewed him into a shroud made from a scrap of old sail. "Did I not give her my heart and my courage and my wit and my eyes?"

"Mm," said Vitrine, stirring the pot so that the neglected stew would not stick. "You gave her your viciousness, and then you threw her mother into the sea. That seldom works out."

"Still, I gave her all of me, the best of me," said the pirate king, his voice muffled now as the laundress stitched the sailcloth over his face.

Vitrine tasted the stew, enjoying the warmth of cayenne, cumin, and cinnamon before it was overwhelmed with the heat of the bird's eye pepper. Even dried and shipped overseas, it was enough to make her fan her mouth and leave the rest.

"You did," she said, because she could be kind. "And she will be magnificent, I promise, and so will the city."

The pirate king might have had more to say about the matter, but then his shroud was sewn up, and he could speak no more. The princess had arranged for her father to be buried at sea, his bones cast from the ship only when there was no shore in sight. When his sail-shrouded body fell to the bottom of the sea, the wythen would clip the stitches with their sharp shell knives, and they would draw him out to serve them forever in their silent crewes. They said that the crewmen told each other stories in the endless nights of the abyssal depths, but it was not Vitrine's concern, and he passed from the city and its story with the soft rasp of oars in their locks and the scrape of a needle through canvas.

Now Malabec Mercer was the richest woman in the city, young and savage, and she set out to conquer it with her embroidered pockets stuffed full of bloody gold. Her father the pirate had had pretensions of respectability. He had hoped one day to immigrate to distant Kailin or Madran, places far more civilized, to live out a genteel retirement. Malabec, on the other hand, had no interest in gentility or foreign lands, no love for sky-loving towers or a dozen generations of inter-city feuding.

Instead she opened her house on Clayborn Street to the world, inviting the scholars and artists that she had learned about through her distant and fearful tutors to come and stay. As she composed her letters, Vitrine sat at her elbow, reminding Malabec of names she thought she remembered, suggesting that this architect might be swayed by the promise of a house of his own, or that singer might appreciate a place where no one cared if he took other men to bed.

They came first in a trickle and then in droves, and when Malabec turned some of them away for being less than she hoped, many of those still went on to settle in the city because it wasn't as if it had been easy for them to get there. Some fell in love with the city just as Vitrine had, and even the ones who didn't gave it a kind of glamour with how much they despised it. It was a kind of hate that almost looped back to something like love, and Vitrine forgave them for it because she understood passion.

Vitrine rather thought that she could get nearly a century out of Malabec, turn her like a jeweled knife to carve the city into shape, but as it turned out, Malabec's taste in lovers proved fatal, much as it had for her own mother. Her fine composer from Byleth slit her throat and then drank poison in a murder-suicide that would be turned into dozens of plays and songs in the next century.

Vitrine looked over the mess with dismay. The plays would never capture the stench of blood, the way the curtains had been half pulled down in the brawl, the graceless sprawl of limbs and the carpet half pulled over Malabec herself when her lover could not bear the sight of her dead.

Vitrine scowled, giving the composer a good hard kick as she went by. To Malabec, she was kinder, flipping the carpet off her surprised face, straightening her limbs to give her a dignity that she had never cared about in life.

The composer's ghost fled to haunt the third floor for some while, and Malabec herself had flown on immediately. Her head, crowned with intricate braids that showed off her fine high forehead and fierce eyebrows, was as empty as a broken-barred birdcage, and the spirit inside had gone elsewhere. Vitrine inspected the inside of her eggshell skull, splashed with outrage and impatience, and with a sigh, she kissed the dead woman and straightened up, stepping neatly around the growing lake of blood.

As she turned, Vitrine took on a severe gown in rusty madder and neat shoes with wooden heels. Her hair, usually kept shorn close to her head, assumed a more demure series of braids than Malabec's own. By the time she was facing the little girl hiding in the corner, her face barred and numb behind the strings of the great Madrani harp, Vitrine was wholly human, stern and protective as a nunnery. There were already strange things fluttering through the child's heart, and they could turn into terrible shadows if they were left to themselves.

"Come out," she said firmly. "That is over now, and you must come out."

The child was still for a long time, long enough for the blood to get sticky, long enough for the composer's limp arm to fall off the writing desk. Still Vitrine waited, because Malabec's daughter needed to see that her new governess could wait forever if she needed to, would, if that was what it took.

Finally, she crept out from behind the harp and put her small sweaty hand in Vitrine's, following her down the long midnight hall.

First they would need to call in the ashmen to take care of the composer's body—she did not need to see him again—and then it would be time for Malabec's wake.

Vitrine got a pang at that, more than just mild regret and irritation at the upset of her plans. Malabec's wake would go on for a week, her body dressed in silk, and her glass coffin, so very like the glass cabinet where Vitrine kept her book, would be set in the hall to oversee all the fun.

Oh what a fine time my princess will miss, Vitrine thought, and she glanced down at Malabec's daughter.

"Tell me," she said. "Do you know how to dance the ganli?"

She waited as the answer swam up through the girl's cotton-fogged mind, and when she shook her head, Vitrine took both her hands, facing her in the front hall.

"They will dance this to mourn your mother," she said. "Best you know how to dance it as well. Look, toe touch the ground, heel touch behind, and left and right . . ."

Soon enough, the little girl was dancing with her, her face still so ashen but two bright smacks of color high on her apple cheeks. She did not smile, which Vitrine would not ask her to do, but her feet were as light as her mother's and her grandmother's had been. Demon and girl danced the ganli, and when they were done, Vitrine clasped her up in her arms and hugged her tight, for she had, all unknowing that night, exchanged her mother for the rule of the city.

THIRTEEN

Vitrine worked for decades without raising her head. Some of the work she did with cart and hastily broken feral horses, perhaps the children and grandchildren of the bay she had sent up the river. The work strained her muscles and left her skin as dry as ash and peeling like diseased bark, and sometimes she went to stand in the mud of the river so that she could remember that she was indeed a living thing that could bend without crackling.

After the buildings came down, the foundations of Azril had been bared, and there were a few surprises waiting for her when she uncovered them.

One day not long after the equinox, when the days were clipped shorter and shorter, she found the sigil of one of her brothers etched in the stone underneath the city. The pavers and packed dirt and then the real soil had pulled back like lips from teeth, and in the pale and gleaming bedrock underneath, she saw a series of familiar curves that made her eyes water and her mouth go dry.

A human seeing that name would have gone mad, but for Vitrine, it was only her brother's name, Gallimane, the harvester at the end of the row. At first Vitrine didn't believe it, and she had to clear out all the soil and sediment to reveal his name in its entirety. She stood at the center of a sigil that would sprawl a good city block, and wondered.

Gallimane was older than she was, old enough he might have been her father. He had been missing for some time now, and whether he was trapped, lost, or only sleeping, there were none who could say. He was a favorite of warlords and poets alike, so handsome that people grew sick of the sun for love of him, and so tall he liked to put his hand on the top of Vitrine's skull to show her how very small she was.

She missed her brother a great deal, and she traced her foot along a curve of his sigil, bent down to see if she could taste any of the ash from when it had been burnt. He had been missing for a century or more now, and he might stay gone for twice that, or he might pop up again, full of stories and with gifts for each one of them, good things to eat or to hide or to rip.

"So you were here too," she murmured. "You did not love this place as I did, but you loved it at least a little, didn't you, to leave your mark here?"

He was silent, still missing, and she demolished his sigil, thinking absently that that was why this district always seemed to breed riots. In general, avarice and cruelty would do that well enough on their own, and it was hardly as if Azril was short on those things, but there was always something about Swallow Street and the Hesters that was inclined to crack and let all of the resentment and grief and pain go spilling out onto the streets with the blood and the brains. Once or twice, when it grew very bad, and people threw each other out the windows from nooses made of torn silk shifts, she had wondered if there was something particularly cursed or haunted about the ground, but the ghosts, new and old, were as puzzled as she was.

A year or so later, looking for a place to get dry from the whipping winter storm, Vitrine found her way to a shielded basement on Ouster Street. She had chosen the stairs leading into the ground randomly and she was pleased enough to find a crate of dominion dated to the year before Azril fell. She sat on the clay floor in the dark, burning fresh wood because the old was beginning to rot away, and on the second bottle—grassy, sweet, and imbued with a hint of wood-like grape stems—she was startled to hear the soft and bell-like sound of singing.

When the angels spoke, they could do it from a thousand mouths that were just one mouth. This sound, the words that spoke holy like the buzz of a mosquito in her ear, was one mouth separated from the rest, lonely and calling for so long that it had forgotten it wasn't supposed to be lonely.

Vitrine squinted at the bottle, wondering hazily if she had drunk something that she should not have, drank some more to be sure, and then she fell on the ground, feeling through the tangle of dust and tiny bones and cast insect husks. Finally, she barked her fingers against the lid of a cistern, so long closed up the lid crumbled even as she grasped it. A portion of the lid fell down the shaft, and when she could not hear a splash, Vitrine shrugged and allowed herself to tumble headlong in as well.

This is how you conquer new worlds, she thought as she fell. *This is how you break yourself into a thousand pieces that are all equally wrong and unloved.*

She landed gently because she didn't wish to break into a thousand pieces, and a tingle in her bare feet made her jump.

It was a gnawing kind of ache, one that would grow unbearable if she stood in place for so long, and so lifting one foot and the other, she reached down to touch the ground. Save for the litter she had dropped from above, it was mostly clear except for a fine and granular dust, and when she brought some curiously to her face, she smelled benjamin and balsam, crisp with just a tinge of iron, and the singing grew louder, as if it suddenly recalled joy and what it was for.

"Oh," she said in surprise. "You used to be an angel."

Vitrine hesitated, and then she said the word, the real word for which *angel* was only an imperfect stand-in. The golden dust hummed in joy, giving thanks as much as dust could give thanks, and Vitrine rubbed her fingers clean with a frown.

This block, she remembered, was always trouble. It did not birth riots like the place where she had found her brother's name written; it was trouble of a more inward kind. Like every city, Azril folded over itself and twisted around over the years. More often than it had been anything else, this place had been a bookbinders district. This area bled ink for love, for pathos, for rousing ballads, and for stirring tirades against those in power.

Blood spilled like ink and ink spilled like blood, she had thought more than once. Perhaps this dust that had once been an angel—and what process had *that* been, what suicide, what willing blindness, or what failure—had something to do with it. Nothing of the world could kill an angel, so it must have been his own maker turned against him.

Even from the bottom of a cistern, Vitrine could call the wind, and she did so now, letting it shift the singing dust and ruffle her clothes. The movement of the air felt good on her wine-sweated skin, and she took several long breaths. She considered what it might be like to scatter an angel or what was left of one. Would the blood continue singing its holiness so softly that only gnats and lice could hear? Would it dissipate to render sacred strange and unlikely things?

In the end, she let the wind circle but then sent it to the harbor instead where it would play tug-of-war with the tides. The golden dust she swept up with a common broom and dustpan, taking a certain pleasure in the fact that the remnants of an angel were mixed now with pow-dered mouse bones, cast-off spider molts, and common dust from the walls. She swept everything up into a pile at the center of the floor, and then she summoned the wind again, this time to whirl every grain and every particle into a large glass bottle sitting at the rear of the chamber.

Instead of corking it, Vitrine brought the bottle's narrow neck to her lips and blew hot and careful. At first there was only her breath whistling over the glass aperture, and then she heated the mouth of the bottle so that it went molten and soft, falling in on itself and going shapeless until the bottle was closed off. She had done the job so neatly that the glass below the neck stayed cool, and the curlicue de-sign of the melusine seducing the young monk on the bot-tle's face was entirely intact.

Vitrine held the bottle for a short while, thinking for the first time of the angel, properly, she supposed, *her* angel, out in the world. He had said that he was not allowed to return home, and if she were entirely honest with herself, she had no idea what angels did with themselves when they were not singing praises or raining down fire.

She pondered it as she hauled the jar up out of the cistern and then west to the place the mansions of the great had once been. Soon enough, it would only be the western region of the city. The mansions had gone—the angel's earthquake had left them shattered.

Despite the lack of stone lions and courtyard walls studded with rough garnet, she found her way easily to the burying ground of her far-ranging Mercers and to the place where years before, the angel had buried a crane girl sacrificed to her anger and her appetite.

As she dug a deep hole in the ground, her mouth stung a little as if to admonish her, and she shrugged it off. She was a demon, and she liked the taste of flesh. Of course she would take it where she could, especially when it had offended her.

There was no thought in her head of laying what had been an angel to rest. No, she was a black squirrel scraping out a shallow cache for later. She didn't know who might want dust that had once been an angel, strange and volatile stuff that could sing praises and find delight in the world, but she had the idea that sooner or later, someone would. Then she could whisper in their ear, take their sleeve and draw them to this place that had once been a graveyard and now was next to nothing. She would watch as they dug up their prize, and then who knew what in the world they would make of it, what gift and what disaster?

She thought of Chanda, nurturing her poison, and of Isra, who clung so hard to the bulbs because even if she believed that she could not begin again, she had believed that they would. Vitrine shook her head.

She was no guardian and no gardener, no matter what

she might once have thought. Instead she was a demon, the
demon of Azril, and she planted a jar of singing dust that
had been an angel deep in the earth. When she was done,
she hesitated and laid her hand over it.

Still the dust sang, and she pulled her hand away.

Well, she thought. *We shall see what will grow from that,
won't we?*

FOURTEEN

Honey and the bees that made it came to Azril from Doufun province in Kailin and from the foothills of the Palas, the round-shouldered mountains to the west. The immigrants kept their hives jealously, guarding the secrets of their apiculture with locked lips and turned heads, refusing to let their charges mingle, and so there were two distinct populations, the great dozy bees from Doufun and the quicker bees from the Palas.

Their keepers were long gone, and the remnants of their hives had blended together in very little time, the queens mating with drones from both populations before flying, laden with potential, to the hollow places in the ruins, the empty logs, even the lowest anchoress cells.

The honey they produced was dark and thin with a bitter edge to it. It pleased Vitrine to call it mourning honey when she went to steal pieces of honeycomb from their hives, but it was sweet overall, strange and special.

This new honey would never have existed if Azril had not fallen, and Vitrine thought that properly she should hate it. She should curse the bastard descendants of the Doufun queens and the Palan drones, turn their vivid yellow stripes white, render them blind and deaf so that they would fall to the ground and signal endlessly for each other.

Her grief tired her out, however, and instead she walked up to their hives and broke off pieces of the comb to drink the honey and to chew on the wax and grubs within it. It tasted of something besides her memories, and sometimes, she was all right with it.

She had prised a handful of brood comb from the colony developing in the cell of Mona Delarova, who had been a poor anchoress but an excellent spy. She had dreamed of uniting the north and south of the Angives, and with her prodigious memory and her gift for languages, she might have done it if a sly narrow man had not come to her cell in the night to smother her. Now bees built vast and ponderous labyrinths of honeycomb where she had once rested her brilliant head, and Vitrine found a bracelet of red ceramic beads she had once worn at the join of the wall and the floor.

The beads clacked on Vitrine's dark wrist, and she carried the brood comb to the beach to eat it. The sun was just rising over the horizon, and Vitrine sat on the dunes, staring out at the sun that had, against all decency, continued to rise despite everything.

The sun had barely escaped from the sea when there were sails on the horizon, and Vitrine rose to her feet with a frown. They gained the bay as she watched, and she saw that these were no towering merchant vessels, no fast pirate coursers. Instead there was a homely humiliated quality to these ships, their sails ragged, a list to their wake that made her think that their rudders must be damaged. There were not many, no more than twenty or so, and the wind that blew them to her smelled of fire and of misery, a hundred nights of bad sleep and more than a year of tears.

So what, Vitrine thought peevishly. *I have had more.*

She stood on the beach with her arms crossed over her chest, her chin tilted up, but to her surprise, they did not land. Instead, the ships turned away, their sails flapping as they drew into the bay but no closer.

A figure launched itself from the first ship, gray wings pearly in the spreading light, and her lip curled as the angel crossed the water and landed where the waves lapped up on the sand.

"Has it been fifty years already?" she asked.

"Fifty years and four days. I was kept back on the veld of Abyssos."

"What kept you on the veld of Abyssos, and why did it not keep you longer?"

He shrugged, his broad hands spread open and his pale palms flashing in the light. He was tired, wavering a little on his feet. His wings weighed him down rather than carrying him up. He was missing some number of feathers on the right, the spaces between them ragged and accusing.

"What always happens when kings want more. It has to come from someone, and when it cannot come from their own people, it must come from other kings. They went to war. They burned down the cities, and the gardens of Igomto are salt fields where nothing will grow again."

"I liked Igomto," Vitrine said without thinking, and then she scowled because it had given the angel some kind of hope.

"I have people here," he said, pointing towards the ships. With their prows turned away from Azril, they had the appearance of children, too nervous to ask for what they needed, tattered and shy in their own want.

"I see that," she said cuttingly. "Is this the best of the lot? Did you winnow them for goodness' sake and this was all that remained?"

"This is all that remained, good, bad, and indifferent," the angel said. "Their families died and they were the ones who got to the harbor fast enough, who got lucky, who happened to be in a place where they could watch the invaders fall upon their families with farming scythes rather than falling under their scythes themselves."

He paused, his throat working. If she tuned her ear to listen to him, she could still hear his praises, but she wondered if they were fainter than they had been before.

"They need a home, and every city needs people," he said at last.

"Ask me."

He bridled at that, because even among angels who were not used to asking, it seemed that this was a particularly unaccustomed act to him. He demanded, he ordered, he bargained, but asking was a new thing, and she stood immobile as he fought with himself.

"May these people land on your shores?" he asked finally. The words came out slowly, and then with greater speed, and it was not until the last that he was able to meet her eyes.

"May they be welcome here and find some shelter from the sea and the storm? May they stay for a while at least so that they can rest and remember how to be people again? May they be unafraid here, as they have not been for months? Many of them are nothing more than broken edges. Could you give them a place to grind those edges down so that they may sleep without cutting themselves?"

Vitrine bit her lip, her gaze traveling from the ships to the angel to the ruins behind her to the angel again. They weren't her people, none of them. They were from somewhere else. They wouldn't sing the same songs or dance the same dances, and she did not love them at all.

"Beg me," she said obdurately. She needed time to think, and she certainly could not do so while he towered over her.

Despite everything that had gone before, the angel hesitated. They both knew that he could force the issue if he wished. He could protect the people aboard the ships from the mischiefs that a demon could do. He could bury her in the mountain to keep her cries from awakening them at night, he could simply bear her away to some distant land while they became the new people of Azril, and it would be another city entirely by the time she found her way back.

Instead he went down to his knees, his splendid wings spread flat to the sand and one hard fist planted on the ground in front of him. It made something in Vitrine stutter as she looked at him, her breath caught in her chest as he raised his eyes to her.

"Please," he said. "Please let them come, please let them live."

"They'll only die on my shores. They'll find the land too harsh since the city fell, the river still too stingy with fish. They'll sicken from the still water in the city wells, and they will fall into the crypts that break open from time to time. They will sicken and die here."

"It is what people do, I am afraid," the angel said in a tone that was perhaps a little too respectful. "They die. I

imagine the people of Azril did it as well, even before my
brothers and I came."

"They're not *my* people," she whispered, gazing at the
ships. She tried to summon up the fury that had been so
very easy to find in years past, where everything that was
not what it had been had sent her into a fit. Where was that
anger now that she needed it? It seemed to have abandoned
her completely, and then the angel reached forward, greatly
daring, to snag a fold of her loose trousers.

She flinched, but he did not reach for her flesh. He only
looked up at her, eyes as deep as the most secret cisterns in
the city, mouth as soft as innocence and likely as breakable.

"Please," he repeated. "Let them stay."

"What will you give me?" she blurted out, and he smiled
as if he had won.

"What do you want?"

*For you to have never come across the sea. For you to have
remained away with your mouthful of praises and your heart
like an empty hall of marble and light, sealed up and inviolate
with nothing of me in you. For my city to be yet standing.*

He knew that, however, and her eyes traced along the
curve of his gray wings instead.

The angel hissed when he followed her gaze, his wings
pulling instinctively towards his body before rising again
in an overt threat. Even on his knees, he looked like the
death of cities, the weeping of mothers and fathers.

"More like a goose than I would have given you credit
for."

His wings might have been gray, but there was a pearl-
iness to them, the very tips of his feathers translucent and
gleaming a dull lilac. They weren't like a goose's wings, or

even like the wings of the imperial eagle, the largest bird on the continent. Instead they were the wings of an angel, magnificent, strong enough to let him circle the world ten times in a thought, powerful enough to stun anyone who got too close. She got too close now, circling behind him to see.

Trembling a little at her own boldness, Vitrine reached out to run the flat of her palm, too intimate by far, along the broad feathers, making them twitch and stir. *He is not made out of earthly stuff any more than I am,* she thought. *Why does it keep surprising me how familiar he feels?*

She grew bolder, ruffling her fingers through the primaries, ticking her fingertips through the finer feathers closer to his shoulders. There were rents in the fabric where his wings pulled through his robes, and through them she could glimpse the dark skin of his back. She had some idea that that skin should be unmarked and clean, but this close, she could see how the salt sea air had cracked it and turned it ashen.

It gave her a pulse of pleasure she wasn't looking for to see him like that, and her fingers tightened on his feathers, taking double fistfuls and making him shift on his knees on the sand. It must have hurt quite a bit even before she tugged, but he made no sound. When she opened her hands, the feathers were bent where she had touched him—one drifted free to the ground.

The angel shuddered silently, his shoulders hunching, his fingers digging into the sand. He wasn't looking at her, and irritated, she came around to touch his chin, tilting his face up. She wanted to see tears, fury, something that would prove what a violation this was. Instead his eyes were wide, and there was something hungry there, something that had entirely forgotten the ships in the harbor and was instead only for her.

Vitrine swayed towards him. Another moment, and she would have seized his wings again, bent them, scattered feathers up and down the beach, drowned him in the water and washed the sand with his blood, and it would have had nothing to do with Azril before or the Azril that came after.

He'd let me, she thought exultantly, and that pulled her back, because she didn't want him to *let* her do anything.

Without her hands on him, the angel looked startled, hunching down closer to the ground as if she might pass him by, a beggar ashamed of his circumstances. The word *ashamed* rang in her mind like a bell, and she reached out again.

"I want them," she said, touching his wings gently.

"*Both* of them?"

"What are you going to do with one?"

There was suddenly a tightness around his eyes, something slack and disbelieving in the hang of his jaw. He looked like he had when she had first cursed him, and the pleasure of that made her smile.

He started to rise. Vitrine could see that as proud as he was, and crafted as he was, most bright, most powerful, he wouldn't, not for a pack of ragged humans, no matter what they had survived or what might become of them without a place to land.

No, the angel wouldn't do it for them, but . . .

"*I* want them," she said. "I want them both. I want them to be mine, and look, I will put them in the glass case inside me, right alongside my book. They will be as important, as treasured."

They would be treasured as war trophies. She would take them out on the longest night of the year to stroke. She would show them off to her elder siblings to make them proud of her. She'd let her younger siblings touch them. She did not know if he understood that that was what she meant, but then none of it mattered any longer because he nodded.

"They're yours," he whispered, and she was so delirious with delight and victory and vengeance that she bent down to slide her fingers through his hair and press her forehead against his. Their breath mingled, and when he closed his eyes, his eyelashes were long enough to graze her cheek as she nuzzled his face.

"Mine," she said with something like reverence. "I will take such good care of them."

She did it with a flake of flint she carved from a boulder on the beach. The waxy gray stone was struck with tiny, terribly keen crescents along the cutting edge, jagged like teeth, and the angel stopped breathing when she passed them over the place where his wings joined his flesh.

Angels, she thought as she did it, were tangles of sense and spirit, never sure if they were flesh or if they were something higher. He had wings sometimes, and some- times he didn't, and all that mattered to her was that after what she did, he would no longer have them at all. They would be hers, and a familiar greed overcame her as she cut them away carefully. It was like cutting clouds, like singing in sudden disharmony, like throwing precious jewels into the sea, and, towards the end, a great deal like deboning a chicken. It was flesh from fat from gristle from bone, and what was left behind was tears and a flood of golden blood on the sand.

The angel crouched down on all fours, his forehead pressed to the ground, giving the earth the soft cries that he didn't want to give to her. Once, he struck the sand with his fist, and when he lifted it, a small crater of glass was left behind, smoking with his rage and his helplessness.

It was long, difficult work, slippery. She cast one wing down on the sand, and immediately went to the other because it seemed to her a worse mutilation to leave the work incomplete. When he would have raised his head to look, she cupped her hand over the back of his neck, pushing him down again.

He doesn't need to see as well, she thought for some reason, and she went to work on the second wing.

It was almost sunset by the time she was done, and she was splattered with gold up to her shoulders and all down her front. She went down to the water to let saltwater clear away the worst of it, blinking at the ships that still lurked in the harbor. It felt to her as if they were ghosts from long ago. They were wraiths from the time when the angel still had both his wings and when she was not as satisfied as she was in this moment.

Why, they are survivors just as Azril is, she thought.

The angel lay curled on his side on the beach, so still she might have thought him dead except for the way his eyes were locked on her every move. His blood was, unexpectedly, drying black, and it soaked his clothes. A single rivulet had made its way over his shoulder and around his neck like a mourning ribbon around the throat of an unlucky girl. Without thinking, she reached to touch it, maybe to smear it, and his teeth snapped. She pulled back, because all right. She had not asked for his blood.

Some few steps away from him were his wings, still beating weakly without anything to glorify or gratify beyond her pleasure. If the rumors were true, they might join with the angel again if they were brought close. He might be whole again someday, but Vitrine doubted it. He might become whole again, but he would never forget that he had been torn or who had done it. Even now, his wings dimmed as she picked them up and placed them with care into her glass cabinet. They rested comfortably next to her book, the gray feathers curling gently against the sides, a drop of golden ichor hanging from a shining knob of bone.

"Well," she said presently, turning to the angel.

"Well," he echoed softly. He had staggered to his feet, and there was a sickness in his face, a tilt to his stance. He looked afraid to take the first steps without his wings, and Vitrine nodded with something like kindness.

"I will go tell them it is safe to land," she said. "This cove is well sheltered from stones. They will be safe here."

"Will they?" he asked hollowly, and to her own surprise, Vitrine reached out to squeeze the angel's hand, pulling away as soon as she had done so.

"They will receive no harm from me. No help either, but no harm."

In the guise of a crane, she turned away from the angel and winged across the water. As she circled the ships, she examined the brown faces that turned up to follow her flight. Soon enough, Vitrine thought, they would know her better, but right now, she was only a wonder, a messenger, a good omen when every hand in the world had been turned against them.

She circled their masts three times, and then with a high whooping cry, she flew back to the city. The ships turned to follow her, and by the time she returned to the bank, it was empty except for a few splatters of ichor and the honeycomb dropped carelessly from her hand.

FIFTEEN

Vitrine kept her word, mostly. For the first few years, she ignored the people who had come to the shores of Azril, and they, in turn, stayed out of her way. They looked upon the crumbling ruins with suspicious fear, instead building shelters down close to the river. Their songs and stories, when they were not too tired or grieved to tell them, were all about the places that they had come from, and Vitrine was not interested in that at all.

She was more concerned with a clowder of cats that had come to take residence that year. They were solid with muscle and large enough that at first she thought they were wildcats that had come down from the hills. When she walked cautiously among them, however, their tufted ears flickered towards her and their kittens pawed lightly at her feet, eager to resume the contract that cats had had with people for some time now.

"Where did you come from?" she asked, holding one calico kitten up to her face. "Did you come with that dull lot on the river? Did you descend from the northern mountains? What could you be?"

The cats acted as if the city was theirs from the beginning, but the angel was more wary. She thought that he might guide the newcomers through their wanderings in the haunted wilderness, but he was as shy of them as he was of her. Sometimes, when she was growing up some blackberry canes or rescuing a cat from some precarious perch, she saw the gleam of something holy out of the corner of her eye or glimpsed fog moving as though it were a man, but that was all.

He wasn't always in the city, but he was there more often than he wasn't, and slowly, in a way that she hadn't previously, she grew used to him the way she grew used to the people on the river and the cats that she knew hadn't lived in the city before.

Still several years went by before Vitrine saw him directly. One evening as she carried a bucket of clams from the water, there was a light among the apple trees that grew where the mansions had once stood. The fruit was at least what it had once been, or it was close enough that she couldn't tell the difference. It was fall, and the apples, red streaked with gold, not much larger than a child's fist, had started to fall to the ground. Soon the boars would come from the high ground to forage for them, growing fat on the fermentation in the rot, but tonight, there was only a soft green light bobbing among the trees. Vitrine tilted her head curiously and went to look.

Between the bent crowns of two trees almost beyond bearing, she found the angel knelt down, one hand touching the ground in front of him, the opposite arm around a lean and frowsy little child. The light she had seen was a clutch of lovestruck fireflies, gathered to adore the angel.

"See," the angel said, "there was a crane girl once, who

I made and who is gone now. She sleeps here, under the stone. Look, take your finger and trace the letters in the stone. They are almost too worn to see, but you can still feel them."

The child, the wooden beads in her hair clacking as she lowered her head, traced the characters on the stone, her lips moving as she tried to give them voice.

"Before it sheltered a worthless crane, it was the grave marker of the fourth Malabec," Vitrine said, coming out of the shadows. "He was a Mercer, one of my favorites. He loved so many men that he emptied the family vaults, and he had to turn pirate to fill them up again."

The angel stood and turned, holding the child more tightly against his body, but the child only looked at her with curiosity. Her face was delicate and round, and there was a determined set to her chin that would incline her towards defiance.

"He said there was a demon in the ruins," the child said. "Is that you?"

Vitrine laughed in surprise to be recognized after so long a time. It had never been very common even in the old days, and when she saw that she had given offense, she bowed to the child.

"I am the demon of Azril. Who are you, so that I may know who to curse if I should ever need to do so?"

The angel bared his teeth at her, and Vitrine observed that there was something desperate to him. He was ragged for all that he still wore a handsome man's face, for all that dust and mud were ashamed to soil the hem of his robe. Here and there, his clothes were still stained with blood, as if water could not touch what she had put him through. Perhaps he wondered if she would ask him to kill this girl as well so that she could eat her over the fire.

The child had no such reservations, and she squirmed out of the angel's arms to stand on her own two feet. She was even shorter than Vitrine had thought she would be, but fearless, and Vitrine grew more interested.

"I'm Jinan, daughter of Ghada and Zolah," she said. "My eimi is a witch, and you can't curse me."

"Imagine that," Vitrine said lightly, not agreeing or disagreeing. "But that headstone that belongs to Malabec Mercer rests over the body of the last girl who displeased me. Would you like to hear Malabec's story instead?"

Story was the magic word, and when the girl nodded, Vitrine looked over her head to the angel, who was wary but calm. Perhaps he was even a little satisfied.

The darkness came on, and over the fire, as the clams she dug steamed in her bucket, she told the girl about Malabec Mercer and the real Avaline Demorsico, and once she had spoken about the Mercers and the Demorsicos, of course she had to speak about the Adebayos as well, who had brought sleek desert horses to the city, breeding them against the sturdy northern horses to make a mount of surpassing strength and beautifully sweet temperament. The Adebayos had lived in Azril until the very last, the night of the angels, but she never got that far in their story, instead telling the child about Kola Adebayo, who had swum his favorite mare out to sea to have her covered by one of the stallions of the sea king Bellam. The union produced the great mare Ba-Dalih, who Hanyo-from-Kittiwake rode to warn the coast of the coming of eastern raiders.

When the clams popped open in the steam, Vitrine plucked out the meat for Jinan, giving her the most savory, most delicate bits. The girl, she could see, was used to being fed thus by her parents and relatives. She accepted the choicest morsels as if they were her due, and she never troubled herself with feeding any to the angel, who watched from the shadows with patience.

"Come on," he said, after the shells were empty and the girl had started to yawn. "Your parents will worry."

"They should. What company their girl keeps," Vitrine said, but the next evening, she went to find the angel.

He stood up to his waist in the water, staring out at the sea and the encroaching darkness. She knew he heard her steps, but he did not turn, and she sat on the shore, her knees drawn up.

"Why did you bring her to me?" she asked at last.

"What makes you think I did?"

Vitrine picked up a stone from the beach, throwing it at him lazily. She didn't mean to strike him, and the stone hit the water by his side. The angel didn't flinch from the small splash or turn towards her.

"You were not made to lie," she reminded him, "and you do the trick of lying without lying very badly. I'll ask you again. Why did you bring her to me?"

"Parents introduce their children to the dangers that they will face. In the southern seas, they teach their children to watch for sharks and squalls. In the north, it is bears and blizzards. Here, it is you."

Vitrine considered, because it was an answer, even an answer that had some truth in it, but it was not the full truth, and she had already decided that she would not accept less.

She pitched another rock at him. This one landed closer and still he did not turn to face her.

"Try one more time," she suggested, and the angel shifted. In her chest, his wings stirred restlessly. If he still had them, he would be aloft and gone from this discussion that he clearly did not want to be having, but he didn't. They were hers, and he had to stay where he was.

"Jinan's parent went into labor a week after you permitted them to land," he said at last. "They gave birth to her under a shelter of woven branches while loons cried over the river and while they were still eating the food they had taken from home."

Vitrine was silent, and the angel, unable to fly, traced a fidgety flaming pattern in the water at his side. It was gone almost as soon as it appeared, but if she closed her eyes, she could see an impression of the mark he had made in the darkness.

"You're saying she's mine," she said at last.

"I'm saying she's her own," he said sharply, looking at her over his shoulder.

"But."

"But she was born here, not in her parents' home, not on the sea. She opened her eyes to see the sun shining over the ruins, and she knows not to eat devil's daughter, no matter how pretty the berries."

"She belongs to Azril," Vitrine said, a pain like an iron spike through her heart.

"She belongs to herself," the angel said sternly, and he walked back to the shore. Vitrine stayed where she was, her back straight as she sat on the sand. She had had a throne for a little while, some few ages ago. She did not care for it the way some of her siblings did, but she remembered what it was to sit with the weight of a nation on her head and the expectation of thousands hanging from her skirts.

"Well?"

"Well," she said slowly. "They are not what I imagined, but I have imagined very little over the last while. I have been more occupied with memory than I have with what comes next."

"It's come now," the angel said shortly. "Now what will you do?"

Vitrine climbed to her feet. She wondered, brushing the sand from her trousers, if she should gain a foot or so in height so she could meet the angel eye to eye, but it had never mattered before. She doubted it would matter in the time to come.

"Give me, oh, let's say three months," she said. "I am out of practice with people. Then bring them in."

"And how shall I do that?" asked the angel with an overly solicitous tone that she chose to overlook.

Vitrine shrugged, already walking back towards the city. She could feel his eyes on her back, and she put a jaunty swing into her hips.

"I am sure you will figure it out, angel," she said.

෫෪෫

Three months later, just as the sun set behind the mountains, the people from Igomto raised their heads at the scream of an eagle sitting in the tree across the river. Its feathers were the white of blasted desert sand, and its eyes were two drops of black volcanic glass.

They came out of their homes to marvel at it, to debate in hushed voices whether it was a good omen or a bad one, but then Jinan shrieked with delight, hopping across the river by the broad stepping stones like a little goat. Her parents ran after her, and so did her aunts and her uncles, and after that, everyone left came along as well because it wasn't a story that one cared to be left out of.

The white eagle screamed as Jinan drew near, and then it winged its way through the pines towards the ruins of the dead city. Some would have turned back when they saw where the eagle wanted to lead them, but Jinan was heedless, following it through the cleared rubble.

She followed the white eagle through the darkening city, her people behind her, and then they came to a plaza where the ground was mosaicked with river pebbles. Fresh water bubbled out of the ground, so clear and cold it made those who went to drink laugh in delight. The plaza was surrounded by a low wall, and set on the wall were stacks of fresh flatbreads, dusted with red salt and still warm as if they had come straight from some diligent baker's oven. The people marveled at the wonder of it, tasting the sweet water and taking ravenous bites from the bread. Soon enough they found the baskets of apples as well as the barrel full of saltwater and clams, and a joyous wondering cry went up.

The eagle landed on the angel's bare arm, her enormous talons digging cruelly into his flesh as he preened her crown. He praised her skill and her beauty and then he threw her aloft before he came to stand next to Vitrine, who was showing Jinan how to sign her name in her book. He waited until Jinan's eimi called her off, and he came to sit beside Vitrine on a fallen column somewhat back from the light.

"Bread and salt and water," he mused. "Graveyard apples and fresh clams. This wasn't what this place was before."

"Well, we're going to have to wait a while for the sweet-breads stuffed in songbirds stuffed in chickens stuffed in ducks stuffed in geese."

"Is that really a thing you did?" asked the angel, momentarily distracted.

"Oh yes. That and strips of raw jellyfish and roasted eel and horse meat charred and served sizzling . . ."

"What I meant to say is, bread and salt and water. It means something, doesn't it?"

Vitrine tasted ashes on her tongue, and abruptly she spat.

Together they watched as the people ate their fill. Fires were lit, giving them light to talk and to laugh. Jinan sat between her parents, her father picking in wonder at the iron-red salt, her eimi tearing off bits of flatbread to give her just as Vitrine had fed her steamed clams. They wondered out loud at the quality of the bread, how white it was and how free of grit, how it tasted just like what they had had at home and had not thought that they would have again.

They wouldn't, either. Vitrine had contracted with some of the winds to bring the grains to her from overland, watching for weeks as they had filled an old brass casket for her. She found the jade mortar and pestle somehow untouched in a buried midden, and they wouldn't put their own grit into the flour like granite would. The red salt she had gathered from a cove up the coast. It was the farthest she had gone from the city since, but coming back with fist-sized lumps of garnet-colored salt had been worth the dizzying nausea and the flood of tears.

"This isn't *their* bread," she said in defiance of Jinan's parents who said that it was. "It's mine. We made it in my old city. I had a mind to make it again."

"The grains won't grow here," the angel said dubiously, breaking one of the flatbreads open. "They won't be able to make it the same as it was."

Vitrine wondered if this was some angelic trait, to find fault with every little thing. Everything where he was from was perfect—did they think it must be so on earth as well? She shook her head in pity. Good luck with that.

"This is where I decided that Azril would be mine," she said. "This was Gallowscross. There were three dead people hung up right over there, and we danced together before they moved on. The Black Dog of Aile came for one of them, Jonavan-in-Fur for another, and the third went with Shining Grace just before dawn."

"An unlucky beginning," the angel said disapprovingly.

In response, Vitrine pointed into the crowd where there was another figure as unseen as they were, shrouded from head to toe in rags of burned linen and with a muzzy veil hiding the place where a face would be.

The figure passed through the celebrating crowd, and Vitrine and the angel both tensed as the fluttering rags brushed past Jinan's cheek. Vitrine had never fought with a psychopomp before, and even if she won, it was widely reckoned a bad thing for demons to quarrel with death. Fortunately, the figure did not pause, instead coming to stand over a woman who sat at the edge of the spring, her face tilted up to the sky and her lips wet and red. The figure hovered there, waiting patiently, and Vitrine nodded.

"Not unlucky at all, angel," she said. "One thing leaves, and another comes."

One city falls and another rises? whispered an insidious little voice in her head, and she shook it off.

A sudden thumping made both of them look up. It was a likely looking young woman with a frame drum, an excited look on her face. The drum looked new, and the drummer did too, new again after what had come before.

She must have left her old drum behind, Vitrine realized. *She should have new and better here.*

There was no reluctance, no hesitation. The beat went on, two short and one long, and then the people from the ships were on their feet, taking hands in trios and dancing in small circles to the rhythm she set. One voice rose up, high and warbling, and others came to join it.

"I know this one," the angel said unexpectedly. "They danced it in Alisar by the sea. I was there for a while after you told me to leave."

"You went dancing? You?"

He frowned at her, but, she noticed with some interest, his fingers tapped out the rhythm against the column down by his hip, where perhaps he thought no one would notice it.

"There is no rule against it."

"No, it is only that I can imagine you taking your place among the men with their leather trousers and the women in their embroidered dresses. You must have looked like a goose honking and flapping your way through the measure."

"I did not. I am—"

He cut himself off, and Vitrine wondered what he had been about to say, whether it was that he was not a goose, or that he was above such taunts or even that he was quite a good dancer. He looked like he was going to be sullen at her, which she could never abide, so she nudged him shoulder to shoulder. There was something softly stinging where they touched, pain meant to admonish both of them to remember their places, but she ignored it, and so did he.

They watched the humans spin and dance, and Vitrine found herself thinking not of how they'd danced in Azril before the end but of the stars above them, their paths so fixed from night to night if you only had a human's short span to watch them. From her vantage point and from his, however, they whirled like Azril's new people did now, catching each other by the hand and circling one another until one or both extinguished, swelling redly before subsiding into coals or shedding their fire in one great breath that stunned the other dancers around them.

Vitrine tilted her head back, gazing up at the stars. They looked the same as they had before, and she pointed to one of the brightest.

"There. Do you remember that one before she took the north? Before every ship in the sea set their prows by her light?"

The angel glanced up, inspecting the star where she shone.

"I do, and I remember the ones that came before him. He has held the honor for some while now. He holds it well."

He pointed in his turn at another star, sparkling modestly closer to the jagged black tree line.

"There. He'll be the next to guide the world."

Vitrine exhaled sharply with annoyance, edging back from him again. Of course he could not talk of such things as a normal person would.

"And when she does, I shall speak of her. Honestly, angel, can nothing be good enough as it is? Can we not love things for what they are while we have them?"

The angel started to answer her, but then there was some upset among the crowd, Jinan fallen down among the dancers and cutting her lip open. She started to cry, and her eimi came to scoop her up in their arms and wash the wound out with water. Jinan cried as if it was the worst thing that had ever happened to her, and Vitrine realized with amusement that it was.

"Do you love them?"

The question took her by surprise, and she looked at the angel narrowly, but he was only looking at Jinan, already done crying, already darting back among the dancers and taking their hands to make herself a part of their whole.

"Of course I don't love them yet. Love takes more than just a good party and some apples. Love takes lifetimes."

"It doesn't. Not always."

The bitterness rose up in his voice like the taste of clove through sugar candy, something sharp and significant. She liked him best with it, because sugar alone was so dull and plain and because once you have mixed a drop of clove oil into a vat of sugar, nothing in the world could take it out.

"No, not always," she said peaceably.

The dancing continued, shifting to the rounds where everyone took hands, those who could stand and those who couldn't, swaying and singing. Vitrine's vision blurred, and she saw a time when the rounds would be larger with more people, and then larger yet, great enough to circle the whole of Azril-that-was and more.

The new people of Azril laughed, embracing one another, and someone came up with the last bottle of liquor they had brought from Igomto. They passed it around, and eventually it came to Vitrine's hand. She took a curious sip, and then a deeper one at the green and herbal taste. They could duplicate it to some extent with the plants grown on the mountain slopes. Perhaps she would wander up tomorrow and see what she could find.

She passed the bottle on, and then the music changed again, and she jumped.

How did they learn the ganli, she wondered, but of course they hadn't. The beginning measures were the same, but the tune hopped like a rabbit, becoming something other so quickly that she made a face. Still it was a good song, and she watched as the crowd rearranged itself, dividing into pairs before taking hands to face each other.

"Do you dance?" the angel asked.

She almost said yes, because this was close, so close to what she had danced before the fire. She would pick up the steps right away, she would kiss her partners and give them dreams and nightmares that would live in them forever. Then she shook her head proudly, leaning back as if the fallen column were a throne.

"Better than anyone you have ever seen," she replied. "But not with you."

The angel might have responded, but a girl came up to kiss his cheek, whirling the angel away. He was not quite as hopeless as Vitrine had guessed he might be. The girl made up for his lack of grace with her own, kindly slowing for him when he stumbled, muscling him through the paces where his knowledge was incomplete.

In the morning the girl would remember that she danced, but not with whom. The work of her hands would be good, and when a pot was thrown perfectly or a kid birthed healthy, she would think of that person she couldn't remember and wonder.

Vitrine watched them spin, all of them, and her toe, all on its own, tapped on the ground. She refused to heed it. It wasn't the ganli, and she wasn't ready to dance something that wasn't the ganli yet.

SIXTEEN

Jinan grew up and grew well, if more reckless than anyone liked. From her father, she learned the writings of what he called their home, and from her eimi, she learned about the weapons that had been used to drive them away from it.

The bread and fresh water brought her people across the river to live in the city, but they did not wander within it, muttering about ghosts in the old lanes and peering at them from around strange corners.

Jinan, on the other hand, went running through the city as often as she could, and as the well-loved daughter of the whole community, the hope of a world to come and the first sign they had that they might be allowed to continue, she was indulged even when she came back with tales about a cat-eyed woman who told her the best stories.

When Jinan was sixteen and her people had built stone houses as well as ones from wood, three ships came up the coast, raiders who were sometimes traders, bearing wealth from cities across the sea. Vitrine followed them in the guise of an osprey, flitting from one bow to the next for almost four days before she made her decision.

The wind whipped up out of a calm night sky, and the sailors found their ships pushed across the rough waves as if by some giant hand. When they tried to sail crosswise out of the edge of the storm, the winds tore their sails to rags and the hulls shrieked as if the wood had learned to fear pain.

The storm broke the ships to bits, another world smashed to birth something new, and in the dawn, the sailors came dazed to shore, clinging to barrels, to spars, one to the mermaid figurehead that had broken cleanly from her ship.

On a sandbar, neither land nor sea, Vitrine stood next to a figure who loomed over her, his skin the cool gray of a sky wondering whether it should storm, his teeth the sharp splinters of broken masts.

"Well, will this do?" he asked as the woman clinging to the wooden mermaid stood up and stared warily at the people coming down from the ruined city.

"It might," Vitrine said, ignoring the baleful glare of the angel who watched from up the beach. "They are good-looking people, don't you think? And strong with the possibility of being generous."

"I hardly trouble myself with such things," her brother said loftily. "I have taken my allotment into my navy, and I am content. And you?"

"Oh, it's a little early to be thinking about navies," Vitrine said absently, but she was suddenly taken by the idea, ships in the harbor equipped with battering rams made from smoke-hardened wood and laminated bone, underwater spikes affixed to innocent-looking merchant vessels.

"No, I meant to ask if you are content or could see yourself to becoming so. You have been quiet for some time now, keeping too close to yourself."

"Not everyone wants to be one face in a crowd," she retorted, an old argument, and her brother laughed.

"Then come be one face at a coffeehouse or on a burning rampart," he said. "I know I am not the only one who has wondered at how you have been."

When she hugged him goodbye, she could hear the bells inside him, enormous sonorous things that rang even deep beneath the water. His own city had sunk, she remembered, and she hugged him a little tighter.

"Maybe," she said.

❧

The people from the sea were a motley lot, some from Combes, some from Mato Lorno, a scattering from the broken states of Brokkslevan, and one rather confused cleric from the distant land of Tuyet, a talking shrike their only companion. Some of them were eager to set off for home, the shores of Azril-that-was too strange and haunted for them, but more decided to stay. The goods on the ships had been promised to wealthy men who did not easily forgive, and Azril's ghosts and her resident demon were not so very terrible.

Jinan took for her lover the woman who had come to shore clinging to the wooden mermaid. At first Juana's stories of the sea and of the distant lands that lay beyond them were only meant to charm the laughing girl with the long braids into her bed. Soon enough, though, she was drawing maps and teaching her new woman the traders' tongue, which would let her bargain for a bag of iron ingots and insult someone's mother almost anywhere she could sail on the White Sea.

At first Juana thought Jinan's interest was only a girlish

fancy, and then she thought it was an obsession, and then one night as she slept on the beach, after a demon came to whisper in her ear, she caught the dream herself. Ambition was contagious, she decided, and she threw in with Jinan and some of the others, children of the first settlers who craved different skylines and different ghosts, people from her own ships who missed their homes.

They had no true shipwrights, but between logs hewn from the forest and the remnants of the ships that had brought them, they crafted something seaworthy. Juana's mermaid was proudly placed on the prow of the ship, and before they set sail, Vitrine reminded one of the sailors that a sacrifice of a small life to the sea would smooth their passage. The sailor wrung a chicken's neck and threw it into the water, and after that, they were on their way.

"Are you going to see her go so easily?" the angel asked as they watched the mustard-dyed sail disappear over the horizon.

"Of course not," Vitrine said, staring after them as if she could unbend the world and see them a little farther on their way. "The world is large, and she might be taken by pirates or an accident. She might drown or fall or falter. She might find some other place she thinks she loves as well as Azril."

"What a shame that would be, to fall in love and be made to stay."

"I love her," Vitrine continued, still watching the empty horizon. "Her name is in my book."

"And you let her go."

"There are many ways to love someone."

Ships bearing refugees and immigrants and traders and scoundrels trickled back along with messages from Jinan, and Vitrine and the angel read them avidly over her parents' shoulders. She was in Johari where there were canals instead of roads, and then she was in Mato Lorno, where they danced with fire and sometimes married their brightest young man to the eternal flame.

Ten years in, she sent back a disgraced mercenary company, soldiers who had fought for the wrong king and now needed a corner of the world where they were not so famous. Vitrine found it at once comforting and disturbing to see swords carried in the city again. Azril-that-was had had navies, both formal and built piecemeal from pirate fleets. On the landward side, the great families had always maintained their own personal armies, both for fighting abroad and for fighting at home.

"She has dreams of empire," the angel said dourly, and Vitrine frowned.

"It's too early for that," she said, "much too early by far. Azril isn't ready to be an empire. It wasn't even ready for that before."

"What do you expect to happen when you tell a girl she can have the world?"

"I told her she could have Azril, which is better," Vitrine said. "Anyway, have some faith."

"In what?"

"In her. I do."

Jinan sent back people who knew how to make fireworks, people who came with cocoons of sleeping mulberry worms sewn into their hats, people with broken hearts and broken heads, cracked just enough to let the light come in.

The first anchoress arrived, her hair cut to a glittering silver stubble and the words of a mad desert god on her tongue. It wasn't quite the same as the god they had worshiped before, but it was close enough, even if it made the angel restless.

Vitrine had become accustomed to the angel coming and going. He might be in the city for a few years at a time, and then through some summons she could never detect or an instinct for wandering that angels unexpectedly possessed, he would be gone, hitching a ride on one of the traders that sailed up and down the coast.

She would oversee the great water wheels that the Attar family wanted to place on the river, and he would be gone. A while later, after trying to figure out what silkworms would eat, she would look up and see him sitting at the fountain or hovering over a blacksmith at the forge. Ten years after Jinan left, she found him standing on the cupola at the top of the new watchtower looking out to sea.

"However did you get up here?" Vitrine asked, shifting from a crane to a human. "Don't tell me you found another set of wings."

"I climbed," the angel said. "Would you be jealous if I had found myself new wings?"

She ignored him, looking out over the water.

"Did you see her?"

"I'm not always on city business, you know," the angel said with a touch of irritation. "I have my own work, and it takes much longer now since I must walk."

She waited, and he sighed.

"She's in good health though abysmal spirits. Juana left her in Padri."

"Oh. Oh, hm."

"I don't think it will last. They've fought before."

"And she's in Padri. They have good food there, and a very fine tradition of assassins and perfumers. Maybe she'll send some back."

Vitrine sat on the edge of the cupola facing the town, her knees drawn up to her chest and her toes dug into the ridge of decorative copper stripping around the edge. It was so new that it had not yet had the chance to go green. So many things were new now.

"I don't know about any of this," she said, spreading her hand to encompass the city.

"No?"

"They're laying the streets all wrong. We used to have wide avenues, so broad and open that you could pass easily and still have plenty of space for vendors. These new streets, they're so narrow, and people are going to start stopping them up in order to charge for passage. Do you know that they are building a wall to the west, a wall with four gates to protect the city? We never had a wall before, not like that."

"They're new. They're just building as they need right now."

Her hand hovered over the town. When she looked between her fingers, she could see the streets that were of course too narrow, the weavers' square that had sprung up where they used to do bear baiting, the hundred and one little things that rubbed at her like a pebble in her boot.

"I just don't know. Perhaps it would be better to start over now, while it would be easier to get it right."

From behind her, the angel affected a cough.

"You know, where I come from, it's widely held that this, all of it, is just beginning. Perhaps it might be forgiven for being only a beginning."

Vitrine froze over like a lake in sudden winter. If she turned to look at him, she might go into a rage, the kind of fury that would rip and tear until it was forcibly stopped, because there was no longer any way for her to stop herself. The wind that blew in from the sea reminded her that he had come over the sea as well, and the warmth of the hearths of the town rose up to her hand, recalling flame.

Then she put her hand down. Without a word, she stepped over the edge of the cupola, letting her crane wings bear her skyward on the updraft.

Let him climb down, she thought. *Let him crawl for all his days on this earth, and may they be long and terrible.*

But she let the city stand as it was, with its misplaced quarters and its narrow crooked streets and the gods that were slightly different from what they had been.

§

It took Jinan twenty years, but she returned at the head of a small swift fleet laden down with a wealth of gold, an ark's worth of seeds and sprouts, a few adventurous scholars, and a new baby.

To Vitrine's delight, she brought with her a pair of Mercer siblings, boy and girl, barely older than Jinan had been when she left. They were darker than her Mercers had been, but Vitrine recognized their cleverness and their ambition immediately. She wondered if one of them would care to change their name to Malabec, because there were some things she missed no matter what came, but for the moment, she installed them in the rookery at the north end of the city, where they might grow up strong and bright and dangerous.

Jinan came back missing some of the optimism she had left with and her right arm above the elbow, and while her parents wailed over the loss, she was philosophic. Vitrine came to see her in the night, standing like a shadow by the hearth of the fine house her riches had built.

"Welcome home, dearest," Vitrine said, and Jinan rose to meet her, pulling her into a hard one-armed hug.

"I thought I dreamed you," Jinan said. "Where's the other? I thought if you were real, he must be as well."

Vitrine ignored her, pacing through the room to see the treasures mounted on the walls and stacked on the shelves. There were tapestries dyed bright gold and red and a sword she had taken from a robber king. There were the horns of a musk ox carved with the story of the great tiger of the Carcanet Mountains and a small box with a winding key that would play a preserved kind of music, never-changing and stale.

"You have gone so far and done so well, but I am so very happy to have you home."

"For a while, anyway," Jinan said, pacing in front of the fire. "It's not as I remembered it. I am not sure it fits me any longer."

Vitrine turned, the skull of a great jungle cat in her hands.

"Of course it does," she said with surprise. "You were firstborn here. Your name is in my book."

Jinan shrugged restlessly, rubbing the stump of her arm. "It's smaller. And colder."

Vitrine drew back, unaccountably hurt.

"Well, it will grow greater. And it's winter right now, of course. You've not had a proper Azril summer since you left."

Jinan smiled at her, leaning back in her chair. She had a sailor's roll to her walk now, and a broadness through the thigh and hip that Vitrine hadn't even guessed at when she was a girl.

"I've lived more of my life away than I have at home."

"But it's still home," Vitrine insisted. "It is. You sent back so many wonderful things, brought so much to this place."

To me, she didn't say.

"You're home now," Vitrine said, hating the hurt in her voice, but Jinan met her eyes with an almost uncanny steadiness. For perhaps the first time, it struck her how long Jinan had been gone, and further, how long it was for a human. Twenty years passed no more swiftly for a demon than it did for a human, but for a human, it was enough time to grow, to change, to learn to want entirely new things and to forget others.

"I'm in Azril now. I'm happy to be here. Juana wants a good place to raise little Elena, and my people are here."

"But?"

"But my people are out there as well," Jinan said, and the way she said it, kind but firm, reminded Vitrine of her gentlest sister, who slithered close to the earth and kept in her chest an apple of surpassing redness wound about with a long lock of black hair.

"They're not so wonderful," Vitrine said, and Jinan shook her head.

"They are. Come. I will tell you about them. When I was away, I wanted to tell you about everything I saw and everything I did. Will you let me?"

It was a bribe, Vitrine saw at once, a placation offered to an old auntie who had grown querulous as the sun went down. She should have spat and cursed Jinan, ungrateful girl with a city she didn't want, terrible betrayer, but she took a deep breath and sat down at the chair opposite Jinan's instead, holding the jungle cat's skull to her as if it was a baby. She stroked the dome of the brain case, teased her fingertips over the sharp edges of the orbital bones that once cradled the great green eyes.

"Tell me about this one," she said finally. "Then tell me everything."

Jinan laughed and did as Vitrine demanded, spinning stories about tall towers that flung fire and fields of white flowers that grew only on the battlefields in the south, their very roots nurtured on the blood of the fallen.

"I want your child," Vitrine said as Jinan's stories drew to a close. It was almost dawn, the sky outside the window pane more gray than black.

"You can't have her," Jinan said with a shrug. "She belongs to herself."

"Still. She has people here, your parents, people she hasn't even met yet. Wherever you go, send her back here. Just for a year, or even less than that. Only make sure that she comes sometime."

Jinan regarded her curiously. In a few hours, when the glamour had worn off the night, she would wonder again whether it was really the demon of Azril that she had talked to or if it was just a dream, vivid and drawn whole cloth from coming home.

"What will you give her?"

Vitrine laughed, happy and pained at once.

"What do you think I will give her?" Vitrine asked, waving towards the window.

"The city. You would give her Azril."

"I gave it to you as well. It's still yours," Vitrine couldn't help pointing out, and Jinan inclined her head graciously.

"All right. No matter how far we go. A year."

Jinan opened her eyes, blinking in the faint morning light. She hadn't been to bed all night, and a little guiltily, she went upstairs to find Juana still asleep, tiny Elena snug in the cradle by the bed. When Jinan came to settle beside her, Juana's dark eyebrows relaxed into gentle curves and her mouth loosened, suddenly easier.

Jinan stroked Elena's downy cheek before coming to rest behind Juana, who still slept badly. Something tugged at the back of her mind, itchy like bad wool, but then it was gone, and she fell into a deep sleep.

On the roof, Vitrine watched the sunrise, unblinking, and the angel climbed up the side of the house to sit next to her.

"It's still her city," Vitrine said mutinously, and the angel shrugged.

"It belongs to many people," he said, and sighing, she nodded.

SEVENTEEN

Jinan and Juana left for Mato Lorno when Elena was two years old, and so they were gone when plague appeared in the city eight years later.

It began with one ship carrying a wealth of copper into port, and it spread like fire had through the streets, the richer parts of the city first, and then the poorer, trickling down as fast and as generously as money never did.

From the wall they had built to defend against raiders, Vitrine watched invisible imps racing through the streets, their faces red and ink on their fingertips, marking doors for the ones who would come after them. First the cough, then the fever, then the swelling at the throat and the eyes and the groin. A slow decline and then a fast one, and soon enough, the gravediggers had formed their own guild, fighting with the young Lord Mayor who demanded a grave and a shroud for each death, even against the swelling tide.

Vitrine, who had better eyes than most, saw the scrawny figures of the plague lords walking the streets, finding the doors that had been marked for them. They entered, and they performed their deadly business, and they bowed to the birds that let them in. Vitrine could see that as well, how the illness traveled in the flights of pigeons that were kept in the dovecotes. Pigeon meat was cheap and savory, and their eggs sold by the quarter- and half-hundred count. Their feathers filled mattresses, their dung nourished the gardens, and they passed the illness to their masters who in turn passed it back to them.

She watched grim-eyed and cold as the illness hid in first the pigeons and then the people. Just when it was isolated on one side, it leaped to the other, and within just a few cycles, the dead were piled high in the graveyards, and the gravediggers and the mayor left off their fight.

There could be no dignity for the dead when the living lived so close and in such fear of them, and so they were thrown into the deepest quarries. In the years to come, the old mines would be reckoned haunted, and from the depths would come terrible and ragged cries for help.

Please. We are here. Do not forget us. Do not leave us. We are here.

The living and the dead were matched in this regard, and as the plague stretched out like thread spun from a bale of good wool roving, that was the refrain that was murmured and sung and shouted and cried throughout the city.

We are here. Do not forget us. Do not leave us.

I never will, Vitrine thought with a soft and sorrowful tenderness. *Whether you were here short or long, I never will.*

The angel found Vitrine sitting on the edge of one of the city wells, dressed in a winding shroud. One end was pulled over her head like a scarf, and she was wrapped down to her ankles, only the tops of her bare feet visible.

"What will you do about this?" he asked. "Or are you a different kind of demon than I supposed?"

"I am no plague lord," she snapped, "and if you knew anything about cities save the destroying of them, you would know that."

The angel pointed west to the district they now called Albemarle.

"Four more died in the night," he said. "Two of them were a couple, and they left behind a baby and one scarce older. None will take them in a time like this, and they will die as surely as if the plague lords had kissed them."

The angel pointed north, where a number of people from Kailin had come to settle. They raised green and blue lanterns over their beds to turn their faces pale, hoping that Lord Mhai, who ruled over the sea at the end of the river, would think he had already taken them.

"They sing the healing songs there during the day. They sing them so much and so often that the holy meaning has gone out of the words, and they are just noise. That is what the children who survive this will remember, noise and death."

The angel pointed east, to the docks.

"They will shoot our ships out of the water, those that still have enough crew to sail. There is already talk from Canna and from Seillon that they will barricade us in if we will not do the proper thing and die before we become their death as well."

"I have heard the talk in Canna and in Seillon," Vitrine said, gathering her shroud around her more tightly. "They are calling it a judgment. It seems that I have heard that story before, angel."

"This is your city," he said. "It's yours, take care of it."

"What do you expect a demon to do?" she said, and she

let him hear the worn threads in her voice, the places where time and sorrow and wrath had made her what she was.

"Aren't your kind meant to be more clever than this?" He glared at her, and she thought momentarily of what he would look like trying to breathe out of a whistling hole in his throat.

"At least my kind are more than a mindless scourge!"

"Cruel," he said, looking up at the houses where the shutters had been daubed with bright blue paint to ward off the illness, and after a moment she realized he wasn't speaking of her. One of the plague lords, skull-headed, fingers long and many-jointed, prodded at the blue paint speculatively, wondering whether it should be denied. A cooing from inside the house, a brace of racing pigeons bought in better times, made the thing nod its hoary head, and it slipped between the gaps in the shutter like so much smoke.

"If you could fix this, you would have, wouldn't you?" she asked, and he was silent. "If you could fix this, I would let you go. If you could . . . speak to someone. One of your brothers, perhaps. Even my siblings who don't care much for me would—"

"We are not like you," he said a little angrily. "We no longer speak."

"Ah."

"Once they might have, but."

He shook his head and she wondered at what might have come after, but he turned to the well, gesturing to the winch.

"Will you hold that for me?"

Curiously, she nodded, and as she held the winch steady,

he put one foot in the wooden bucket and one hand on the rope.

"All right, now lower me and slowly if you please, without jokes."

"I do not make jokes, angel," she said with dignity, but perhaps she found a wry and wicked smile at the idea of consigning an angel to the pit via a series of slow half turns of the winch. Inside her, his wings beat anxiously, and she hummed as the rope jerked back and forth before he called to be lifted up again.

He was muddied when he rose up, soaked up to the knee, but he stepped off the edge of the well, dumping out the pail full to the brim with small drowned animals. No one had been fishing them out, and people would drink bad water before they would go without.

"Is that all you can do?" she asked, shaking her head, and he shrugged angrily, wringing out the hem of his robe.

"My skill set is very limited," he retorted, just as a flight of pigeons broke cover overhead.

They watched as the flock wheeled over their heads, their wings flashing gray and green and white and pink in the sun, and then disappeared over the city.

"Hmm," they both said.

༺༓༻

The next sunrise saw the dovecotes a place of slaughter. The feathers floated down to produce a soft bloody mat on the ground, and every bird was dead. The cry went up from district to district, echoing and panicked and grieved, and the plague lords took it up as well, a hollow and high-pitched shriek of disappointment.

There were only two pigeons left in Azril, a crowned white and an almandine racer, their bellies heavy with the plague and their eyes as bright as jewels. Vitrine had taken them from the dovecotes of a messenger service, separating them carefully from the flock by virtue of the identifying sigils on their leg bands. She released them from the watch-tower, unmanned for half a year now.

The crowned white flew on the west wind to Canna, and the almandine racer made her way down the coast to the tall steeples of Seillon. Vitrine watched them go, pulling her dark red shawl a little more securely over her head. She had pinned it with a delicate iron brooch shaped like a crane in flight.

Cranes suit the city better than pigeons do, anyway, she thought.

They would eat the cranes in the time to come, bereft of squab and the plump layers that put out two eggs every three days until they died. They might eat the mangy cats and dogs as well, and, perhaps if things grew terribly bad, even each other.

However, as she walked back to the city center, the plague lords and their red-faced imps flew over her head, their diaphanous robes blotting out the waning sun and leaving her in momentary chill as they passed by. She lifted her hand to them, for even if they were not her own family, they were likely kin of one sort or another.

She watched until they were out of sight, some gone over the sea, some gone down the coast, and then she made her way into the city, where they had built great fires that stank of burning feathers and tortured meat.

She found the angel sitting next to some of Juana's cousins, politely holding a mug of beer as the humans fell down drunk around him. Their doublets were covered in down and their hands filthy from the day's work. In the morning, they would remember that there had been five on their crew, but when they tried to name each one, they would only come up with four.

"Well, they were happy for the extra hands, anyway," he said. "Though I can't do much with the beer."

"A shame for you," she said, taking it from him and drinking it down with one gulp. She smashed the mug into the fire and lifted one of the drunks into her arms, half carrying him, half dragging him as she whirled around the flame. He pulled away in surprise, but somewhere else close by, the exhaling notes of a set of pipes floated to them, fast and very good. The musicians had had a difficult time. They'd become gravediggers and professional mourners, but soon there would be a day when people would need music more than they needed either.

"Come and I will teach you the ganli," she said to the men. "I danced it for three dead at Gallowscross and for so many after. You will love it, I promise, and you will want to dance it all the days of your life."

The men groaned in exhaustion, but one, short and fat, came up to his feet and took her hands in his. She laughed with delight, and she wondered if she had danced with someone like him sometime in the past, caught his face out of the corner of her eye or seen some great-great-great-grandparent succeed or swing. Then it didn't matter because she was dancing with him now, and he was a good dancer.

She danced with him, and then when she reached for another partner, so did he. They pulled others and others still into their orbit, something like a plague itself, and some drums joined the lonely piper. They thought they danced for death, but Vitrine knew otherwise. They always danced for life, no matter how death lapped their heels.

Vitrine turned and came face-to-face with the angel, standing on the sidelines like the disappointed girl at the party. She looked up at him, not enjoying how much taller he was, and then half haughty, mostly convinced he would refuse, she offered him her hands, palms up. To her surprise, he didn't hesitate a moment, though he held her hands as gingerly as if they were hollow-boned birds, biting his lip hesitantly.

"Doubting yourself already?"

"Only in that I do not know this dance." Then, more defiantly, "It is only dancing."

It was seldom only dancing, but Vitrine did not owe him that explanation. Instead, as the music came around again, she took a step back and the angel took a step forward. Her mind flashed briefly to retreats and pursuits, natural to her kind and to his, but anyway, their roles had never been set in stone. When the music changed, perhaps she would chase him.

"Follow me," she said, and he did, clumsily at first, and then with enough confidence that she could leave off steering him and simply dance with him. Their shadows were greater than the bonfires could throw, and their feet left tender, shallow hollows on the stones where they stepped.

When the rain filled those hollows in the generations to come, they would steam slightly, one of the thousands of small wonders of Azril that would never be remarked or observed.

The crowd unthinkingly made way for them without knowing why they did so, the same way they would resist a riptide or pull back from a hot iron. They recognized Vitrine and the angel in their spines and in the spaces between their shoulder blades and in their skin, and they danced with them like they danced with the threat of drowning or burns.

The steps, it occurred to Vitrine, were not quite the same as the dance she remembered, too fast, a hop where there should have been a pause, and too short, as if there was a bit missing, but she didn't care. They were dancing the ganli again in Azril, and right in that moment, every pigeon in the city dead, the plague lords gone on to other places, and an angel holding her hands, it was all right.

EIGHTEEN

Alex, first named Elena, returned to Azril as a heartbroken, furious teenager, dressed in a pair of stolen trousers and with his hair cut short. He had stowed away on a ship from Combes only to be discovered as the ship was making its way into the harbor.

Drawn in by the shouting, Vitrine, in the uniform of one of the harbor masters, came up to take Alex by the arm. At the captain's protest, she cut him down with a cold look.

"This one is under my jurisdiction now, and as far as Azril is concerned, so are you."

The captain, who wanted to see Alex hanged, pulled back in chagrin with a sullen *yes sir,* and Vitrine briskly marched her new charge into the city.

"Where are you taking me?" Alex demanded, trying to sound bigger than he was. "I'll crack your head open, I'll slit your throat."

"Well, where would you like me to take you?" Vitrine asked, and he blinked, because now she looked like a middle-aged auntie, comfortable in the tunic, loose trousers, and shawl that were so common in Laal. Laal and her famous princess had recently awakened from a two-hundred-year sleep, and were finally trading with the world again.

"Let me go," he said in sudden terror, and Vitrine did, causing him to flail back into a pretzel seller carrying her wares on a forked pole. When it looked as if he was going to do as poorly with the pretzel seller as he had with the ship's captain, Vitrine stepped forward again, purchasing two pretzels from the irked vendor and handing one to Alex.

"There," she said. "It's good, and that's the second time I got you out of trouble. That's two more than most people get from me."

Alex, half the pretzel already in his mouth, looked at her apprehensively.

"What happens if I get in trouble again?"

"If?" Vitrine snorted. "I don't think *if* is the word you want there, my lad."

They ate their pretzels leaned against a broken wall that had once marked Azril's boundary against foreign mercenaries, where they had to surrender their arms if they wanted to gain the city's center. Some of these walls had survived the angels, but there were fewer of them than there had been once. They'd been dismantled for stone, and now people used the old markers and boundaries as doorsteps and foundations.

"These are good," Alex said reluctantly, and Vitrine smiled. They were, new and good both, and she was coming around to them.

"So what brings you to Azril?" she asked companionably.

"A promise to my mothers." When he saw that that would not serve, he sighed.

"They told me that I must spend a year of my life here. I don't know why, but I promised them. I promised them right before they—well. It was a promise."

The grief was still new. Vitrine guessed that Alex was no more than sixteen. Sixteen was fragile, and she had never had much use for fragile.

"And what will you do with that promise?"

"Find some family, I guess. Mother said I had family here that would recognize her name and—"

"Oh, they're gone," Vitrine said, watching his face closely. "In the first week of the great plague, them and their household. There's no one here for you."

There was a brief shattering, a child so far from home that he could not take one step further without growing up all at once. Then he pulled himself back together, piece by jagged piece, looking more like Juana than he did Jinan, who had after all been loved every day of her life. No one loved Alex anymore, and Vitrine was still not sure if she would take it up.

"Fine, then there is no one here for me," he said, nothing more than a welter of hurt feelings, and finishing the pretzel, he stalked off.

"He is going towards the Mazes," the angel said with some asperity. "They're going to slit his stomach on the off chance that he swallowed diamonds."

"So he is," she said. "If he comes out alive, I'll find him a nice place to live."

"You could find him a nice place to live now."

"So could you."

The angel gave her a dire look. He would be handsome in the new fashions from Laal, but he insisted on the long tunic and rope belt that the old ascetics wore. Honestly, hopeless.

"Give me some money," he said at last, holding out his hand as if surely she would.

"And why would I do that?"

"Because I am not permitted to steal it, and I am not permitted to earn it," he said sternly. "Because clothes and food and shelter cost money."

"Why?"

He knew she was not looking for a lecture on trade and the violence of those who ate well against those who did not. He couldn't quite meet her eyes.

"Because we loved Jinan, didn't we? We saw her grow, and we saw her off. We'll never see her again."

The wings in Vitrine's glass cabinet stirred, gently, almost shyly, and she pressed her hand over her chest to calm them. She imagined, briefly and disconcertingly, reaching up to do the same to the angel. She wondered what she might feel if she set her hand to the scarring over his heart, whether it would beat like a human's or thunder like the sea or sing like a bird. Perhaps it would only be that stupid humming sound he made when he did not care to argue with her but still wished her to know he disapproved.

Vitrine dropped a scattering of silver and gold into his palm.

"For Jinan, then, and not for you, and not for that boy, not yet. He still has to impress me."

Angels did not roll their eyes, but this one came close.

"I'll let him know," he said, disappearing after Alex into the narrow twisting alleys.

The angel kept Alex alive, and observing from the dark corners and deep doorways, Vitrine could see that that was no easy trick. Fragile, she had thought him, and there would always be something fragile about him in the heart, apt to break, and so cheap he would hand it to almost anyone.

In a mostly futile effort to protect that frail heart, the angel put a sword in his hand, and in the cramped courtyards of the Mazes, under the jeering of the returned pigeons and the girls swinging their bare legs out the windows, he taught him how to use it. Sitting with her arm slung around the shoulders of a girl who would put the whole of the city on its back for her skills on the stage, Vitrine considered the strange pair circling each other below, Alex too eager, the angel already resigned to correcting another foolhardy lunge.

"He's more patient than I thought he would be." Vitrine watched the angel haul Alex to his feet yet again. There seemed to be no end to the number of times he was willing to do it.

"You weren't here yesterday," the girl snugged up to her side said. "The little idiot tried to do some kind of silly jumping lunge and nearly ran himself through. His master turned the air red with curses."

Imagine, an angel cursing. Vitrine gleefully put it away to hold over his head later. Below, Alex went down on his knees, the angel's own sword flicking up to touch his throat, then away. Without hesitation, Alex rose, and the way he called for the angel to come again was nothing short of a command.

His master, the girl had called the angel, but Vitrine doubted it. The angel was no one's master, no matter what fire danced at his fingertips.

Almost as if he had heard her, the angel raised his eyes to find Vitrine sitting on the windowsill, her red silk wrap trailing down the dirty brick like a spill of blood. The part of herself she'd put in him shone, and with a shout of triumph, Alex locked the angel's blade with his, shoving him back two paces and forcing the angel to meet him with a startled cry.

"There," Alex cried, sounding even younger than he was. "And when was the last time anyone forced you to yield?"

"Never save once," the angel replied, turning away from Vitrine decisively. "Here. It doesn't mean anything if you can't do it again."

Alex never could, but he quickly found that fighting men or creatures that pretended to be men was far easier than fighting an angel. The first time he killed someone he ended up puking out his guts in the alley with the angel standing guard over him. On his other side, Vitrine looked him over critically, taking in his bent back and the sweat on his brow.

"He's not very good at this."

The angel bristled.

"Why must he be good at this? What sort of monster should he be that he takes joy or ease in such a thing?"

"Well, perhaps he'd be like you."

"Angels do not take pleasure in slaughter."

It had been some time since they'd spat at each other

like this. Vitrine found she had missed it, and she eyed him with a sharp grin, rubbing Alex's back as he heaved.

"No? We take pleasure in what we are good at, and I have seen you excel at little beyond the ending of lives."

"You know nothing of the purpose I fill."

She pursed her lips prettily, and she lifted her hand from Alex's back only to bring it back down silvered with claws, long ones, hooked, that she had borrowed from one of the deadly smilers, the great cats that haunted the plains of the south. The blow came within a hairsbreadth of the back of Alex's head but the angel snatched her wrist and held it in an iron grip, the look of shock and fury on his face so funny she laughed. Vitrine shook him off, stepping back and sweeping out her skirts like a girl well pleased with the one who'd had her against the wall.

"Look at what a good little nursemaid you are. How skilled, and how caring."

The angel growled, a sound like lions, but Alex moaned, staggering up and wiping his mouth shakily.

"Who are you speaking to? I thought I heard someone—"

"You heard nothing worth hearing. Here. Drink some water."

Alex staggered to the fountain and drank gingerly, nodding when he kept it down. He'd have the scar from the cut scabbing over on his neck the rest of his life. He'd always hear the other man's last gasping breath in his dreams. He would never really feel safe again. Still, he was the same boy, and Vitrine felt a new pang of affection for him. Her city was always her city no matter what had happened to it, and this was still Alex, no matter what had happened to him.

Vitrine put a slip of paper in the angel's hand along with

a scatter of stars made of hammered gold. She'd found them when they were digging out the foundations for a new hospital on the north end of the city. She didn't know whose throat or wrist they had circled in the great long ago, but they were beautiful, gleaming gently in the angel's palm. What an impossible sky he would make, solemn without any hint of dawn or dusk to threaten his constancy. With a night like him, no one would worship the day.

"Here. Take him to this address. He can get food and some sleep in a proper bed for once."

The angel gave her a suspicious look.

"*Only* a meal and some sleep?"

"Well, that depends on what he likes. There's plenty there. Perhaps you will get what you like as well."

"I doubt it."

"If only you could be pleased by something as simple as a brothel. Go on."

The angel might have protested, but Alex looked around in confusion.

"I don't think I've ever seen you look like that before, old man. What moves?"

Vitrine, close enough she could have leaned in to kiss Alex's mouth, smiled with all her teeth bared.

"I do. In the shadows, in the river. In that heart you'll give away over and over again and the pride that you never will. I move, Alex."

The angel snorted, taking him by the shoulder and turning him away from her decisively.

"Come on. You need a meal and some sleep."

She watched them go, absently ducking under the dark winged thing that had come to collect Alex's victim. What a wonder it might be if only the angel could be eased and comforted at a brothel. What the world might look like then.

At the mouth of the alley, Alex glanced over his shoulder, not for one last look at the sorry scene, but because he thought he had glimpsed out of the corner of his eye the motion of a hand, first tipped upright and then languidly laid down, palm up, like a drawbridge. It was a thrown kiss, and the place where the other man had cut him stung suddenly.

Then his priest tugged him back into line and he hurried after, and he never thought about that hand or that kiss again.

In truth, she never intended to look in on Alex as much as she did. She had matters to attend to as Azril grew tall again, ships to send out, building plans to inspect, people to keep or send away, but again and again, she looked around and there he was. It was hard to miss a young swordsman with an angel at his heels, and whenever she sent over a drink or a meal, she made sure it was carried by some interesting, dangerous thing that was sure to capture Alex's attention and to make the angel despair of his charge's chances of living until morning. By the end of Alex's year, he was strong and swaggering, pretending to be the best sword for hire in the city and mostly getting away with it. These days, there was plenty of opportunity for swords and bloodshed. Gold poured into Azril, enough to pay for city guards and mercenaries alike, and Alex flirted with their company as if he was always on the verge of falling in love.

"Well?" asked the angel in exhaustion. He was so tired that he didn't even protest the picture they made, the worn-out mendicant friar sitting down in the tavern with Vitrine in her fine courtesan's dress. His hair was as dark as ever, but she liked to imagine gray threaded through the black, some outward sign of his harried, harrowed year.

"Well?" she echoed, sipping delicately at her drink.

"Well, will he do?"

"Do what?" she asked with interest. "I only asked Jinan for a year with her child. It's been a year. And it looks like he's going to pick a fight with that big man from Yfs. That's going to go poorly for him."

The angel rose from the table with a weary totter, but laughing, she sent the man from Yfs on his way.

Alex came strutting to the table, taking the third chair and giving Vitrine what he likely considered a seductive look. It wasn't bad, but it wasn't good yet, either.

"Well hello, bright eyes," he said, leaning in. "Is my old priest taking good care of you?"

"Let's not talk about your dull old priest," she said, giving him a slow and feline blink. "Let us talk about what you want instead."

"Everything," he said grandly, and it made Vitrine laugh, because she could tell he didn't mean it. When she looked into the chambers of his heart, his wishes were homelier than those of either of his mothers. He wanted comfort and pleasure. He wanted people to know him as a dangerous man, one worthy of respect and fear. He wanted to come home over and over again and to find it just the same as when he left. That last was an impossible thing, and Vitrine set it aside to call for wine and for fish stewed in a clay pot with garlic, sugar, and imported ginger.

"I like the way you talk," Alex said much later, the tavern empty and the pot of fish demolished between them. His dark head rested on the table, his nose just inches away from where the letters *AEV* were carved deep into the wood. AEV had been very bold and clever, gambling with the city cats for their secrets. She'd lost her right eye on the first throw of the dice, and the smallest finger on her left hand on the second, but on the third, she had won all their eyes for her own. Instead of taking them, she'd left them in the heads of the tabbies, the selves, the calicoes, and the tortoiseshells. Whatever they saw, she saw, and she made herself very rich and very dangerous with her hundred eyes.

"Do you? What else do you like?"

"Everything," he said again, and this time it was somewhat closer to the truth. Heart with a wide-open door, poor thing, and as she held the fishbones up to tease the tavern cats, she considered.

"What do you think?" she asked the angel, who sat with his arms folded across his chest. In the light of the banked hearth, his head slightly bowed, he might have been drowsing, but of course he did not sleep. What wonders she might have seen if she had demanded his eyes instead of his wings, but she could not have borne to leave them where they were.

"I think he is drunk, and I think you already know what you want to do."

She started to retort that she had merely asked for his thoughts, not his reproach, but it occurred to her that he was right.

She wanted Alex to have the city, and Vitrine decided that she would give it to him.

Alex took Juana's family name, Lorca, and in a year or so, he managed to catch up to his own reputation. He recruited a mercenary company from his companions in the Mazes, and he fed them well enough that they were only occasionally tempted to bite him. They were savage, and Vitrine was often happier to see them out of the city than in it. Alex ranged inland where his mothers had gone to sea, offering his services to this city or that one, always returning to Azril, which he called the only woman who ever had his heart.

"He's just like you," the angel said in exasperation. "Have you heard his latest poems to Azril's towers?"

"Terrible, simply awful," Vitrine said happily. "And yes, he loves this city almost as much as I do."

Every time Alex returned to Azril, after he had washed off the blood and grit and seen his gold deposited safely in the new banks, he went to the coffeehouse on Marigold Street to meet with his old priest and his first patron, a glamorous and mysterious courtesan.

"You two never change," he said, eating the bowl of rice noodle soup. "Why is that?"

"Would you like us to?" Vitrine asked in amusement, but the angel scowled.

"Why should we?" he asked. "It is enough that you do. You have grown thinner since you were home last, and look at the scars on you."

"I never change, I will always be this strong, this vicious, and this alone," boasted Alex, and because he was her favorite, Vitrine reached out to touch his chin, turning his head to see the woman coming in the door.

She was small and brown, unremarkable in every way save for how relentlessly unremarkable she was. She had taken pains to make herself so, and the business that had brought her to Azril was a bloody one. She was vengeance's daughter, and the knife strapped to her leg, easily grasped through a slit in her pocket, was very sharp.

Then she looked up, meeting Alex's gaze. That alchemy that Vitrine suspected sparked, and fate shifted in its banks.

Forgetting his patron and his priest in a moment, Alex stumbled to his feet, almost tripping over his sword.

"Marry me," he said, and vengeance's daughter laughed straight in his face. Vitrine liked that laugh a great deal. The angel frowned.

"What will you give me?" she asked.

"Anything. Anything at all."

She looked him over closely, and her eyes lit on his sword.

"Are you any good with that?" she asked, and he puffed up like a singing bird.

"The best there's ever been."

"Well," she said, "buy me dinner. We'll talk."

"Oh, no," the angel said. "This will only end in—"

"With good luck and kind fate, it might never end at all," Vitrine said, running her fingers along the bloody threads of the girl's quarrel. "But come along. We're not wanted here."

They weren't, and the angel followed her into the street.

"You can't keep him from every danger," she reminded him. "You never could."

"You don't care about him at all. That girl has blood dripping from her skirts."

"And he leaves bloody footsteps wherever he goes. It's a good match, I think."

"For him or for the city?"

"For me, it's the same."

Vitrine sighed when the angel looked mutinous.

"I shouldn't have to give you of all things a lecture on playing favorites."

He looked abashed at that, and he was not seen in the city for a handful of years. It was fine. Vitrine had things to do, and there was the blood and intrigue that vengeance's daughter would spin around Azril like a spiderweb, giving it a hard and garnet glitter.

Be vicious, be loved, and be lucky, read the words Alex had chiseled over the mansion he built on what used to be Clayborn Street, and largely, they were. When they grew older, they sank into a respectable middle age that they took to quite well, and from the exploits of their younger days, they had a fortune, a share in a fleet of ships, and a pack of children, saved or given or salvaged.

"It's quite a lot," Vitrine said, playing the adoring auntie that of course they all remembered. "Do you have a favorite?"

Alex gave her a wink, holding the youngest on his knee.

"They're all my favorite."

"Are they?" she asked archly. "I thought Azril was your favorite."

"Of course it is. Just like every child is my favorite, and my wife is my favorite, and you are my favorite."

He paused.

"You didn't bring my old priest with you this time."

"No, he is even less constant than you are. But tell me, if you wanted one of these children for your heir . . ."

"One of these children for Azril, you mean," he said, and she nodded.

"All of them."

"Well, of course all of them," she said. "But is there any single one—"

He shook his head abruptly, and she saw the specter of his early years in him still, when she had told a sixteen-year-old that there was no one in Azril who loved him.

"If there must be one, then you choose," he said. "And please never tell me."

She climbed to her feet, taking his hand gently. It was his left, where the joints had grown stiff in the previous year. When he died, he would barely be able to move it at all.

"All right," she said. "Thank you. You won't see me again."

NINETEEN

In the end, she didn't choose, instead writing all their names in her book. They grew, one or two died, and the rest thrived in the streets and courts of the new Azril. More than once, Vitrine came across the angel hurrying after this one or that, sitting at a lawyer's elbow as she argued, keeping a drunken mercenary captain from tumbling into the river.

"I'm not doing anything wrong," he said before she could speak, and Vitrine covered a smile.

"You're not doing anything right, either. That one's a worse murderer than Alex could ever have dreamed of being."

The angel looked perhaps a bit abashed, and Federico Lorca walked on, unaware of the demon and the angel on the bridge behind him.

"I knew him when he was small," the angel muttered. "He was sweet then."

"He's sweet now, if you ignore the dead and the ones who loved them. You have grown strange in the past years, angel."

"I have not. I am not meant to change."

Alex had said the same thing, but it would be, Vitrine

thought, cruel to bring him up. Alex had died the summer before, and the angel was more sensitive to such things than she was. Instead she hoisted herself up to sit on the bridge's stone balustrade, dangling her bare feet over the rushing of the river water.

"It wouldn't be so bad, would it?" she asked over her shoulder, and the angel regarded her warily. Still those same old robes. So dull.

"It's inevitable," she continued. "I had to learn it the hard way. I'm still learning."

"And here I thought you knew everything."

She made a face, turning to gaze at the river. They were preparing for Summersend again, though they called it by a different name. Paper lanterns lit up the banks, and bits of song drifted to them over the lapping water.

"Compared to you, I do."

He came to stand beside her, and the distance between them was less than it had been in the previous decades. It struck her that they were both older than they had been, a rare concept for something as everlasting as they were.

"Is this what it was like before?"

"Do you think I will forgive you if it is?"

His laugh was short and sharp, the humorless bark of a desert dog.

"I know better than to wish for the moon to return to the earth."

"Then what?"

"I only wish to know. Was it this bright, this loud? What does that book of yours say?"

She hesitated, pressing her hand to the center of her chest, and then, almost without quite understanding why

she would do such a thing, she pulled out her book. She
found the page almost immediately, her finger skimming
over the lines as she read out loud.

❧

*Someone has started the tradition of setting little paper boats
on the water, painted with wax and set alight. Every year,
they sail flaming down the river, clustered together before they
sink to trouble the catfish and the turtles. They say that if your
ship makes it to sea, you will have your fondest wish before the
end of the year. They seldom make it past the Third Bridge, let
alone gain the harbor, but still they are beautiful.*

*This year, the boats became snagged on the body of a
drowned girl, foundering on her skirts, trapped by her hair. I
took her back to Calliope's to be treated decently, poor thing,
and she told me as they slip-stitched her lips and her eyelids
shut that her wish was that whoever pushed her in should be
pushed in themselves.*

I was having such a good time, *she told me.* I wish I
could have stayed a little longer.

*Next year, I will have lanterns lit along the banks to call the
people out. There will be musicians and food vendors, whores,
thieves, those up too late and those who have awakened to see
what the matter is. Next year, there will be a thousand little
boats carrying a thousand wishes to the harbor, and I will put
two in the water for her, one for the death of her murderer and
one for her good rest among the reliquaries of Old Rooster, who
ministers the unlucky dead.*

Next year, there will be such light.

❧

She closed the book again, gazing out over the river. She should bring back the feast of the boats, lanterns along the river, wishes traveling to sea.

"I made it bright and loud," Vitrine said. "Before me, was silence."

A low voice carried back to them on the wind, Federico's. He had stopped only a short way up the river, and now he stood on one of the stone piers, singing in a rumbling baritone of the faithful girl and the faithless moon. Somewhere across the river, a light tenor answered him, the faithful moon, the faithless girl.

"Tell me something?" the angel asked.

"If I want to."

"What have I done here? How much of this city is mine?"

Apparently Vitrine was still capable of a red rage, and there was no separation between hearing the question and her hand darting out to grab the angel by his ragged collar and pitch him into the water with an almighty splash. He came up sputtering with surprise, and she snarled down at him.

"None of it!" Vitrine shouted. "Do you hear me, none of it is yours! It's mine, and it has nothing to do with you!"

It was a lie, and she knew it even before she said it, and she thought, watching the smile flicker over the angel's lips by the shattered light from a dozen lanterns, that he knew it too.

On the banks, a pack of children shouted with laughter at seeing someone go into the drink, and they poled their raft to him. When they reached him, however, he was gone, and they sent up a panicked shout at how he might have drowned so fast.

On the bridge above, Vitrine snorted, walking back to the riverbank. Of course there was no argument he could make, and she followed Alex's drunken son until he found his way back home.

There were a few restful decades after that, and then one rather terrible set of years where a religious mania took the city, breaking the windows and burning the old lux- uries. Vitrine gritted her teeth and dealt with it, because such things happened sometimes. The angel stood by with a worried look on his face, because it had as much and as little to do with him as it did with her, and more than once, she caught him staring in shock around him. Still, he held his tongue and so did she, and the bad years passed, followed by the founding of a scriptorium and a university. Azril's reputation for learning and for beauty returned, as well as its reputation for decadence and sex.

Another dozen years, and someone came up with a tech- nique for bleaching stone. Now all the towers that they reared up in the city were white, gleaming, and gorgeous, and in Vitrine's chest, her book bristled with new names. Sometimes she still saw the ghosts of old Azril, but they were happier now, and anyway, they would have been long dead long ago.

One day, watching as Alex's great-granddaughter's fleet left the harbor for distant Sui, Vitrine felt the angel's wings flutter in her chest. She pressed her hand between her breasts, calming them the way she had become accustomed to doing, and she paused, counting.

It had been some three hundred years, she guessed, since. She was never good with numbers. Still, three hundred years was a long time for an angel or a demon. She wasn't in the business of forgiving, but changing, that she could do.

The angel approached her where she stood on the quay.

"There's a unicorn at the market," he said without preamble. "Doan is trying to buy it for the university."

Doan was another one of Alex's descendants. The angel kept better track than she did.

"A unicorn?"

"Yes," he said with some asperity. "The merchant who brought it in has drugged it, or it would have killed half the square by now."

"Oh, I should go see," Vitrine said, and she followed him off the beach.

TWENTY

Shani left Azril with a hundred weight of silver deposited for her in the bank, easily accessed wherever she cared to roam, and Vitrine never found out why she needed it. The only thing she cared about was that Shani, who had earned her place in Vitrine's book after one wild chase across the rooftops when she was fifteen, would return someday and spend a year in Azril. It was a deal Vitrine had struck several times now, and her returners were like presents, delightful things that opened to reveal all the world.

Shani returned to Azril alone, a solitary figure wrapped up in a rusty-red cloak, a pair of spectacles pinched to the bridge of her nose, making her dark eyes appear enormous and quizzical like the eyes of an owl.

Just short of twenty years after she left, Shani came back to the city with a heart half-open, wary of the world around her but ready, Vitrine thought, to love Azril if it would give her the chance to do so.

"She doesn't look as bright as Jinan did. Do you think she is at least as strong?" Vitrine said, watching Shani pass by from one of the balcony cafes that were all over Eastside, which they'd built over Carnelian Street. Across from her, the angel warmed his hands on a mug of tea, considering.

"She reminds me a little of Alex's daughter Zahara. I think she will be as strong as she needs to be."

"As strong as I need her to be?"

The angel laughed, rising from the table and relying on Vitrine as usual to provide the gratuity.

"As *she* needs to be. They don't have to be the same thing."

"What do you know, anyway?" Vitrine said, laying down a smattering of small coins. Some of them bore dear faces long dead, others were clipped bronze, but one, only as large as her pinkie nail, was gold.

"I know that you have been waiting for her to come back. I know that you have missed her."

Vitrine paused on the balcony railing, hesitating for a moment.

"Do you want to come meet her?" she asked, giving no indication of what she thought or whether she would allow such a thing.

The angel shook his head.

"No, I think I'll go see about those crates that are being unloaded off at the rooms she rented. I'll see her sooner or later."

Vitrine followed Shani through the streets in the guise of a lanky black rooster, an enormous and self-satisfied tabby, and a small limping child, peering at her from around corners, from the doorways, and from the alleys. She nodded in satisfaction as Shani fended off a would-be mugger, frowned at how she chose the smallest, stingiest bun from the vendor.

"Hm, I do not know if I care for ascetics," she mused, and Shani shrugged.

"Well, I do not know if I care for the city anymore, so we're even."

Vitrine drew back, woman-shaped, surprised and offended, and Shani smiled, drawing her cloak more tightly around herself.

"I suspected that you were no natural thing when I was a child. I've hardly grown less blind."

Vitrine recovered from her surprise, and she stepped up to offer Shani her arm. Shani was half a head taller than she was, her hair going gray in badger-like stripes from her temples, and she took Vitrine's arm as carelessly as a young girl.

"Well, you are a new thing," Vitrine said as they walked down a street where she had once shoveled bones. "I did not expect someone like you."

"Most don't," Shani said placidly. "I would have come sooner, but I would not come empty-handed. Demon of Azril, I have brought you a gift."

"A gift," Vitrine said, unaccountably flattered. "An offering, a bribe?"

"A *gift*. I will not try to get out of my year here—"

"Get out of!" Vitrine huffed, but Shani only laughed.

"Who knows, I may stay after all and find my true home, if there is such a thing. But I thought I would like to greet you properly, and perhaps to pay you back for a certain rescue on the rooftops."

She led Vitrine back to the rooms she had rented on what used to be Law Street, where the scholars had once played at being fools and the fools had pretended to be scholars. Now it was a wealthy district, and Shani had rented out the whole bottom floor of one of the great houses. Rather luxurious for such a mousy woman, Vitrine thought, but then she saw that almost every room was filled with crates, straight wooden boards all smelling of brief, fast pine and nailed together with care. Shani took a pry bar to one of them, and when the lid was toppled over, Vitrine stared at the cargo inside, cushioned in wood shavings and closed as tightly upon themselves as secrets.

"Oh, Shani," Vitrine breathed, and she took from the crate a volume wrapped in waterproofed paper to keep it dry. It was so new the pages had not been cut, so young that the ink seemed bled into the paper.

"A Natural History of the Glass-Winged Butterfly," Vitrine read. "Oh my darling, is it real?"

"The book, yes," Shani said with a smile. "The butterfly, I suppose you will have to take that up with the author."

She pulled out one book after another, and then when that crate was empty, there was another, and another.

"How did you collect all of these?" she asked. "You must have sacked a city."

"Nothing so exciting," Shani demurred. "There are some people who are tricked, and two or three who are dead. Do you like your present?"

"Ever so much," Vitrine said, drawing out another book, and then another. She forced herself to look away from the books, though she kept a volume on the war machines of Evelyn clutched to her chest.

"What a fine thing you have given me. Still, you must stay the year, though. I love the books immediately, but I would like to have the chance to love you for a while as well."

"Of course," Shani said graciously, and Vitrine warmed

to her manners and her generosity, even if she suspected her of an abstinent streak and a set of scales and measures where other people kept their hearts. What a good thing it was that she had so much experience loving all sorts.

She found the angel a few hours later, seated on a crate at the rear of the apartment and reading a volume of alchemical theory. The book with its red leather cover and gold tooling looked delicate in his killer's hands, and as she hovered in the door, bemused, he spoke without looking up.

"Surely they know it is a heresy," he said, troubled. "Surely they know that if they did this, they would rend the world as we know it to flames and to dust."

"I'm sure they don't know," Vitrine said, prying open another crate. This one held botanical treatises and, to her delight, romances as well, all mixed in with democratic abandon. If she had her way, all libraries would be arranged like this, promiscuous, free to mingle, and truth found everywhere and nowhere at all.

There was a family living in the apartment above, and a rather poor poet in the attic. They would have to go, she decided, though the frail new ghosts that had come to live in the house in recent years could stay. The new library in Azril was going to be beautiful, and if she thought of boarded-up windows and a young man too afraid to venture over the doorstep, it was only for a moment.

TWENTY-ONE

Shani did not stay in Azril, no matter what Vitrine promised her, and the angel went with her when her year was up, taking up a sailor's kit bag and joining the crew as if he was meant to be there.

"I'll stay with her at least until she gains Brid," he said as Vitrine shadowed them down to the docks. They were full again, with pennants and flags from all over the world. It was not what it had been the night the angel and his brothers came over the water, but Vitrine noted absently that it was getting harder to remember that older harbor when this one was so very lively with sailors, smugglers, spies, and soldiers.

"And then where will you go?" she asked, only curious, but it made him smile, white teeth flashing in his dark beard.

"I haven't been away from the city for a while. They surely must have built that basilica in Combes by now, and there's that rumor of the horned white snake somewhere in the sacred springs of Soeur Martine. They say it can heal anything with just the touch of its horn."

"Oh, if you find the snake, bring it back here. It can live in one of the Old Town wells," Vitrine said, briefly distracted, and then she frowned, shaking her head.

"When should I come back?" he asked, and Vitrine shrugged, her shoulders sharp.

"Why in the world should it matter to me?"

"It has never been my lot to question why," the angel said almost primly, and then, softer, "*Will* I be allowed back if I leave?"

Vitrine lifted her chin proudly, crossing her arms over her chest. In her pocket was a palm-sized treatise on the wild horses of Mato Lorno, who traveled the mountains in an enormous elliptical circuit. Every spring found them in the same sheltered valley. Foals born late in the peaks knew their way to this valley, and they continued to know it even when they had been broken to the saddle and the bridle, their shod hooves kicking up anxious and eager sparks when they were ready to go home.

"I don't stand guard on the docks, barring the way to those who come," she said haughtily.

"And if I come through the mountains?" There was a slight sway to his voice as if he had remembered something of the hypnotic nature of words, how a sung chant and re-ply could bury itself in your ear, and then your mind, and then your heart.

"Then you have come through the mountains," Vitrine exclaimed. "What do I care?"

"But you will not bar my way?"

"It is *not* my business where you go."

It looked for a moment as if the angel wanted to say something more, but then he shook his head, and turned, gaining the ship just as the sails unfurled and billowed out with a snap.

She watched Shani watching her from the deck, waving

to each other until the ship was just a dark speck on the horizon. She was waving to Shani, who she knew she would never see again, and of course she was waving to no one else.

For all that she had grown accustomed to the angel's questions and wry comments, she truly did not miss him at all for the first ten years or the ten after that. There was simply too much going on to think of angels. There was a revolution brewing in the city, too short-sighted and too little concerned with material matters to last long, but she thought that they might do some damage that she could ill afford when the city still felt so tender and new.

She watched anxiously as they broke to riots one hot summer day, and in the end, her Azril was not hurt at all, not a single building sacked, not a single plinth toppled. It was something of a successful movement, if she was going to be entirely fair, and it was not as if she liked the companies in town who paid in scrip only accepted by the companies' own shops. She had found the gray tickets for fish and meat and medicine and vegetables to be offensive, a nothing that pretended to be something, and she startled herself by marching with the mob, shouting and fighting and rolling from the heart of the west side all the way to the outskirts of the town where the companies, mining mostly, some ceramics, were stationed.

She thought it would be a rather lot of yelling for little at all, and she had shrieked with delight when they came out and burned a handful of the greasy gray tokens to show that they had succeeded.

Things got better, things got worse. A rainy spring brought a sickness to the water, and many died. Refugees arrived from some war over the mountains, and many were

born. One of them, a fat man with a grave face and dragon-
fire burns up his arms, brought with him bags of ruby frit
and copper as well as a long steel pipe that let him blow
spheres of glass, speckled with red and blue, fantastically
delicate and sharper than serpent's teeth when shattered.

He tempted Vitrine into meeting with him at Pike's
Crossing, which had a reputation for haunted deals. It was
something of a private amusement to Vitrine, because Pike's
Crossing had once been Verdant, the center of the jewelers
district in Azril-that-was, and therefore one of the most
luxurious places in the city.

Still she met with him, and when he showed her his glass,
baubles and goblets and lenses and knives, she showed him
to a certain well where a man twenty years before had buried a fortune. The man had died of a knife to the side of
his neck before he could come back to collect, and Vitrine
shooed his ghost away as the glassblower left with enough
gold to start his own shop.

"Oh shush," Vitrine said to the reproachful ghost. "I
only want good glass in the city again."

Sometime later, when the glassblower's son started to
grind lenses for the observatory that was being built on the
hill, Vitrine found herself wondering where the angel had
gone. His wings in her chest were quiet, stirring in sub-
dued response when she touched them, but otherwise she
had nothing of him, no new citizens, no cunning lanterns
from Muying, no ivory aviaries filled with strange birds or
reptiles.

It irritated her to be so irritated with his absence, and
so for another ten years, she locked away all thought of
him and worked on the observatory on the hill, watching

the lenses grow larger and clearer, bringing the heavens to earth and submitting the decorous stars to mortal eyes.

Sometimes, shortly before dawn, when the astronomers were piled up like puppies in exhausted, satisfied sleep, Vitrine took her place at the eyepiece, scanning the small section of the sky it encompassed. The angel's home was no more in the sky than her own homeland lay beneath the earth, but there was some correspondence, she thought, in the glitter of the fading morning stars, in the way the black became blue with no clear line to divide them.

"They won't let him back in," she said. "They wouldn't dare."

Inside her glass case, his wings—her wings—beat fretfully, and she hummed a soft song to calm them.

"He's not there," she said to the sleeping astronomers. "That means that he's somewhere here, and that's all I care about."

There was actually a great deal to care about in Azril, as the time picked up speed again and the years started to spin around her. There were buildings that wished to go up, and buildings that needed to come down, another spot of plague which was not as terrible as the first but still brought back bad memories. There was a brief trend for stampeding horses through the blocked streets. Of course there was food to eat and fortunes to lose. Someone developed a recipe for fried dough wrapped around salty pork, sweet strips of pickled radish and raw onions, and they were suddenly selling it everywhere.

A dancing girl from Sui awakened the memory of an old promise, and Vitrine went to the greenhouses, upsetting the careful work of the horticulturists to bloom splashy white blossoms in the midst of their reds and blues and yellows. The white flowers had a fleshy translucence to their thick petals, nearly glowing in natural light. They were a great favorite of the churches in Azril, of which there were now several, and after they were cast spent into the trash, they seeded and their seeds took root in whatever soil they could find. In the space of two years, they'd gone from rare to as common as cats. People grew them by their doorsteps, lovers snatched up great handfuls to give to their sweethearts, and of course they were scattered across the graves of those who died nameless in Azril, far from home and uncomforted except for those glorious white flowers.

Every day the sun rose on Azril, and Vitrine forgot that she was trying to bring the city back to what it was. Instead, she threw herself into making it what it would become. It was a labor of love and obsession, a single patch of pavers as likely to catch her attention as Shani's library, now one of the greatest in the region.

The library had become her favorite, and in its roots, she saw the anxious young man who had died with all the rest that fateful night, and also Jinan's need to know the world and Juana's need to weigh it and Alex's curiosity and Shani's cleverness in giving a demon precisely what she wanted.

Vitrine spent a few years as one of the custodians of the books, answering only to the Lord Mayor and funding the collection from the pockets of those who sought its wisdom, but she quickly realized that she much preferred to be a patron.

She had her cell on the third floor, the door gated with a curlicue design of wrought black iron, and when she found something that she wanted to read through to the finish, she locked it in there so it would be hers until she was done.

Vitrine had liked to read before, but now in her library, she loved it, and she began most dawns there, sipping the strong coffee they imported from L'koga and Tesh, reading a romance or an engineering manual or a speculation on the nature of demons and angels. She nodded sagely when they got something right and snickered when they, more often, got a thing wrong.

She was reading when the first cannonball fired from the army come to the gates struck the western wall, and suddenly Azril was at war.

TWENTY-TWO

The demands came the next day, and Vitrine read them with growing horror over the shoulders of the Lord Mayor and the council members. Her Azril, a tributary state? Her city, forced to turn away any ships from Combes, Mato Lorno, Noor, and Padri? Her children, sent to foreign wars and foreign churches? Hers made someone else's?

It was unacceptable, and she had built well and cleverly enough that no one else in the city would permit it either.

The demands went back stuffed into the tongueless mouth of the messenger who had brought them, and the call went out immediately, to prepare for what came next. Leadership of the merchants' private guards was hastily consolidated, trading vessels donned armor plating and rode low in the water.

Before this in Azril, war was mostly something that happened elsewhere, to other people. The old city was great friends with the mercenaries, had allies strung like pearls up and down the coast that loved her and feared each other too much to try to claim Azril for their own. Once in a while, the people would turn on each other, or more often, they would single out those who bore the mark of a foreigner in some way or another, different, too unlike to be tolerated when just a few days ago, they had eaten the same fish, went to the same coffee shops, and danced together the steps of the ganli.

Vitrine was philosophical about the blood that occasionally ran in the streets, but war was something different. War had driven her from Saqarra in the south, which was nothing anymore but jokes for the jackals and tragedy for the historians. Now the cannon fire, the bodies hung from poles, and the full beds in hastily erected infirmaries stirred up things that she had deliberately and ruthlessly forgotten.

What emerged from the muck in her mind, slow-blooded and remorseless as the catfish gods that swam in the river, reached out cold hands and sharp hooks for her. As the siege wore on, she mired in her ghosts, dragged down and made still.

Vitrine's hands were slow when she joined the cannon teams, and when she put her ear to the ground to listen for sappers beyond the wall, the only thing she heard were the commands to retreat in Kanaian, which was spoken in her lost city and had not been heard in the world for four hundred years or more.

I wonder if there are still some nomadic nations that speak it, at least as a trade language, Vitrine wondered, her feet dragging as she walked in the streets. *They were the ones who gave it to us first, maybe they carry it still. Would they come to Azril if I asked, would they bring it here with their indigo dye and their skills with scarification? They were so very beautiful.*

She looked up from her reverie to find that two weeks had passed. Azril captured the general's son, a dreamy-eyed youth who they hanged from the walls in fury and vengeance. It was a quick thing, ill-considered and hasty. In apology, she waited with him on the wall until his mother, dead of devil's daughter poison delivered by a jealous mistress, came to pick him up.

The youth and his mother were exactly what she would have wanted for Azril in better times, and she would have written their names in her book with such beautiful inks if her hand, shaking all the time now, could remember how to write at all.

It was too loud and too bloody for her to take her book out. Her book was too fragile, her hand too unsure. Instead as the war tumbled on, she left it locked inside glass, refusing to add more to it, refusing to let it remind her of what she had written in its pages. She watched in slight befuddlement as the observatory came down, one terrible enemy cannon seeming to seek it out for malicious destruction.

"What a shame," Vitrine said out loud, walking barefoot over the shattered glass and melted brass. The astronomers were covered up with the heavy felt cloths that had once protected the great lenses. The lenses didn't need them anymore, and Vitrine wondered at the water on her face that fell with no rain in the sky.

The war continued. People died, terribly and easily, both those who were mourned and those who were not. Soon enough, the weight of grief blotted out everything that was not rage, and the balance of the two fueled each other, kept up with the dreary cannonade and made the slow starvation of the people of Azril a little more bearable until of course it wasn't. Vitrine could have told them that they could eat only rage so long before it was fatal, but by then, she had stopped talking, even to herself.

Help was coming from Padri. It arrived in the form of a single ship of mercenaries and expectations of extravagant thanks should Azril survive.

Help was coming from Combes, but it was blown off course, or perhaps it was never sent at all.

Vitrine knew that help never came, and as the cold winds descended, the invaders breached the city wall, streaming through the break five hours before dawn.

By then, Vitrine had been sitting on the front steps of the library ruins for three weeks, crouched in on herself, wondering if the sea would take Azril like the sand had taken Saqarra, wondering if this time it would take her too. She curled around the book inside her, still not daring to take it out, and the blood in the streets rose up to lap at her bare toes.

She barely noticed when the most recent Malabec Mercer used what was left of the library for a last stand, and she didn't look up when a gentle hand touched her shoulder, tugging back the wool scarf she had pulled over her head to make sure it was really her.

The angel had to come overland, because no ships would sail to Azril, and coming into the city, he had picked up a sword. He swung it in an arc that reflected his terrible light, and he took the burning fumes of the city into himself with a deep breath, eyes kindling dragons.

"Tell me I can," he said, and for an instant, he thought she was too far gone, too sunk in horror and pain to respond, but she rose, moving like a statue would move if it could.

Vitrine stood on the last intact and unbroken part of the library stairs, and she pointed towards the fighting, her arm as straight as a spear. She could no longer speak, and it was only dirt and blood on her face because her tears had gone somewhere else, but it was enough, and the angel turned.

Vitrine felt his wings beating frantically against the glass, and she wrapped her arms around her chest as if they might escape. She watched as he dropped his human guise, stood up bright and burning as he had so long ago.

Will you give way? he had asked her, and she never had.

He could not soar above the city, but she could no more take away his faculty for destruction than she could take the breath out of the air or the salt from the sea. The sword he carried was nothing more than will sharpened, and death ran after him like a child trying to keep up.

The screams went up, and the tides of the people in the street turned. Vitrine knew that he had been too long away, that he would not always be able to tell invader from citizen, her people from those who had come to conquer them.

The angel walked fast in Azril, and those who were faster than he was gained the wall. They escaped through the breach and through gates both common and secret, they escaped to sea, and he let them go. Those who saw him pass remembered different things, and afterwards they dreamed of him, love without mercy and fury without holiness.

An hour before dawn, an eerie quiet swept over Azril like a velvet cloth over a half-finished game of dominoes. It had never been so silent before except that terrible morning after Summersend, but it was not dead. It was only that everyone who still lived in the city, citizen and invader alike, was crowded as still as stone in cellars, in midden heaps, in belfries, and in barrels. They were made all alike by terror, and in the years to come, it would bind them together until they could imagine no allegiance save what was forged under the fear of the angel's terrible love.

The angel made three rounds of the city, and finally he returned to the library, where Vitrine stood waiting for him.

"It's done," he said, gesturing to the ruin behind him.

Vitrine nodded, because whatever other flaws the angel was prey to, dishonesty was not one of them.

"All right. Do you want to be free?"

She spread her hand, and his wings, faintly pearly even in the darkest part of the night, rose up over her head, as perfect as the day she had taken them.

The angel looked away.

"I don't want you to ask me that."

She folded his wings away again as neatly as a conjurer disappearing a dove or a cartographer erasing a road or a town.

"What do you want?"

It was not, Vitrine imagined, a question that was often asked of angels. She waited and waited, patient as she could be for things that mattered.

"I want," he said carefully, "for you to love me as I love you."

In her chest, his wings fluttered and her book opened, as if a strong and wild wind were riffling its pages. Her book was heavy and the pages, though marked with ink and mud and blood, could bear many more names. When it appeared in her hands, as solid as iron, the angel's head came up, but she closed it firmly, shaking her head, making it disappear again.

"I don't care about your name," she said. "Come here."

He followed her over the shattered door of the library, walking between the two pillars of pink Padri marble, somehow still standing. The foyer drifted with paper scraps as deep as mountain snow, heresies and romances and theological speculations and recipes all mingling with abandon. Resting in one drift of paper was Malabec Mercer, and as she passed, Vitrine straightened his limbs and kissed his forehead. He had been in her book since he was a toddler, and she would mourn him later and ever afterwards.

The library's atrium, wide enough for a dozen couples to dance the ganli without ever touching, rose up three stories overhead, and dead bodies littered the marble floor and marksmen hung dead over the mezzanine railings. All was shrouded with shattered glass from the rose window far above. The window had drenched the atrium in blue and gold light when the sun shone down, but now it was open to the night, the last stars, the scudding clouds.

"Come here," Vitrine said again, and she lay down on her side in the broken glass, the body of a fifteen-year-old mercenary from Noor five paces from her head and the body of a librarian a dozen paces from her feet.

Hesitantly, the angel came to rest on his side facing her. He smelled of sweat and blood, or rather, his clothes did. When Vitrine leaned into bury her nose in his throat, he smelled like a cold winter day, of sunlight banishing rot.

"I don't know how—"

"You'll learn."

She embraced him carelessly, letting the shattered glass cut her bare arms and legs, heedless of the dust that threatened to choke her. She kissed him with hundreds of years of passion, not all of it fond, and she pressed herself to his body, which was for love of her losing its memory of skin and of blood.

"I love you so, I love you best," she whispered, nipping firmly at his ear. "I will walk in you, and I will care for you, and I will bring the whole world to rejoice in you."

The angel sighed, a noise like the turning of pages, like the gust of air closed out of a heavy leather-bound grimoire. He rolled over on his back, his hands down by his sides, and Vitrine found in his skin the brown marble from Padri, in his nails the steel fittings from Combes.

She slid one strong thigh over his, perching on his hips and leaning down to kiss the column of his throat, splitting his shirt to find his skin.

The angel tasted of love and also of fear and of hope, sweet and bitter at once and making her mouth water for more. He cried out in offense when she bit him too hard, leaving a tender spot to the right of where his navel would be, and she laved the stinging with her tongue, not in apology but because bruised flesh tasted good to her as well.

Underneath her, the angel's body grew taut and tense, his hands opening and closing as she kissed him and touched. He was growing colder now, and stretching out beyond her as well, blood and bone and will and fear and hope straining to the limits of his skin and then passing through them. They bound books in human skin sometimes, but angel skin could bind something different, and Vitrine smiled.

"I love you so, I love you best," she whispered, and under her hand, he groaned, shaking with the pleasure that dripped like anchoress honey from her fingertips. She rose him up to suit her expert eye, letting the heat of him, akin to what lit the stars, work to turn bone to granite, blood to wood.

Vitrine's breath caught in her throat as something low and deep in her belly went tense, and she sat up straight, looking at the black night sky in the shattered window above. The circular opening ringed with toothy glass shards looked back at her, and the angel's hands came up to touch her with fearful devotion, sliding over her skin with increasing confidence.

"Oh yes," she said in brief surprise. She would love him, and more than she had thought she would, but that was the way of loving most things. You couldn't portion love out in spoons or cups or slices. You could only let it grow and nurture it if you could, cut it down if you had to.

The angel, stretched almost to bursting already, opened to her with a shy and gossamer flutter, and then she could shape him as easily as her sister shaped her own face, as easily as her brother shaped coral palaces beneath the sea. She wanted granite for the exterior and marble for the interior, she wanted shelves fanned out like the rays of the sun itself from the atrium, which after all was only a chambered heart opening the way to all the rest.

He was open, he was folded and spun and stretched and mauled until there was nothing left of an angel that looked like a man, until the marble floor spread from him like blood and pillars like bone rose up to support the vaulted ceiling. His mouth opened, he cried out, and it was not for holiness but for her, all for her.

Exhausted, filthy, and exalted, Vitrine fell to her back on the cold clean floor, her arms spread wide as if for an embrace, breathing in the air that was heavy with the scent of vellum and leather and polished wood. She stared up at the unbroken window high above, amber now instead of blue, and she smiled because she knew he saw her. She had used his eye to make it, blowing it out with a puff of air until the color was thin but true.

Beyond the walls of the library, the people were beginning to move again, coming out of their hides. They would reckon what they had lost, whether it was to a lovesick angel or to an enemy sword. They would find out what was left, and they would mourn what had gone. Sooner or later, they would begin to repair what was broken.

That was for tomorrow, however, and right now, Vitrine climbed to her feet, looking around at her library with wonder and pleasure. There were very few things that emerged into the world perfect from a dream, but this was one of them, shaped in all its particulars to what she had seen for her city hundreds of years ago. It was a library, and it was an angel, and nothing of this world could destroy it. The city would rise and fall, but the library would stay.

Vitrine smiled, and then reaching past a pair of quiet gray wings, she took out her book. She touched the paper lovingly, flipping from the pages that were marked to the ones that were empty. She would return to write in the book many more times, enough that soon she might need a new book, and she found herself looking forward to it. There were wonders ahead, and monsters and miracles as well.

"I love you so, I love you best," she whispered, three times true.

DAWN

The demon slid her book into its place on the library's shelves, and she walked out into the morning city.

ACKNOWLEDGMENTS

I started *The City in Glass* early in 2020. It's my pandemic book, the thing I wrote while cooped up in my apartment with only my cat for company, and it's just about the hardest thing I've ever written. As I followed Vitrine back and forth in time, through heartbreak and triumph, grief and glory, I learned to sew on a machine, acquired a bunch of houseplants, launched my career in traditional publishing, and thought a lot about the end of the world.

Thanks first go to my agent, Diana Fox, who heard me pitch this book as, "So have you ever wondered if you could fuck a library?" and did not fire me on the spot.

Thanks as well go to Ruoxi Chen, who championed this book through its inception and development, and to Sanaa Ali-Virani, who saw it through to the end. Sanaa, I can't wait to see the fun we're going to have together. Ruoxi, I am never going to forget that you plucked *The Empress of Salt and Fortune* out of the slush pile and changed everything for me. You're the first one who saw that Chih and Almost Brilliant could carry a series, and a bit of that faith will be carried forward in every Singing Hills book to come.

To the hardworking and endlessly patient staff at Tordotcom: Oliver Dougherty, Christine Foltzer, Alexis Saarela, Sarah Weeks, Michael Dudding, Eileen Lawrence, Isa Caban, Samantha Friedlander, Lauren Hougen, Heather

Saunders, and Jacqueline Huber-Rodriguez: thank you so much. I promise I will work on being more timely with my emails.

Thank you to Cris Chingwa, Victoria Coy, Leah Kolman, and Meredy Shipp, you guys are fantastic, and I'm gonna make you all such good food when I see you next.

Shane Hochstetler, Carolyn Mulroney, and Grace Palmer, here's to 2024 and every year after. Wouldn't want to spend it with anyone else.

What I've learned in my forties is that the world is always ending, but if we're tough and lucky, if we only hang on a little longer, go a little farther, fight a little harder, there's a chance we'll be here to see the new one come in.

See ya in the new world.

ABOUT THE AUTHOR

©2021 CJ Foeckler

NGHI Vo is the author of the novels *Siren Queen* and *The Chosen and the Beautiful,* as well as the acclaimed novellas of the Singing Hills Cycle, which began with *The Empress of Salt and Fortune.* The series entries have been finalists for the Locus Award and the Lambda Literary Award, and have won the Crawford Award, the Ignyte Award, and the Hugo Award. Born in Illinois, she now lives on the shores of Lake Michigan. She believes in the ritual of lipstick, the power of stories, and the right to change your mind.

nghivo.com
Twitter: @NghiVoWriting
Goodreads: Nghi Vo